A CONVENIENT
GROOM

A CONVENIENT GROOM

BY

DARCY MAGUIRE

MILLS & BOON®

First published in Great Britain 2004
Large Print edition 2004
Harlequin Mills & Boon Limited,
Eton House, 18-24 Paradise Road,
Richmond, Surrey TW9 1SR

© Debra D'Arcy 2004

ISBN 0 263 18130 8

Set in Times Roman 18 on 20 pt.
16-1204-39823

Printed and bound in Great Britain
by Antony Rowe Ltd, Chippenham, Wiltshire

CHAPTER ONE

'HEY, I lost my phone number...can I have yours?'

The nasal whine to the man's voice didn't give Riana Andrews any encouragement; neither did the pick-up line.

She shook her head vehemently and stared into her cocktail without even looking at the man. She wasn't at this club to get a guy—she already had someone in her life. So Stuart may have said he was too busy to see her this week—she lifted her chin—she was busy too.

She looked at her watch. Where was Maggie? She was meant to be here by now...

Maggie was her best friend-cum-co-worker. She'd persuaded Riana to come to the trendy club to convince a top photographer to rearrange his schedule so he could shoot her gowns. It was cutting it close for time but she needed the work done before her debut into the big world of fashion next week. Everyone would want photos of her designs—she hoped.

She was fine with waiting at the bar, except for the guys with the corny pick-up lines that seemed to be rife tonight. Riana had heard about all the lines in existence and then some in the last half-hour.

She picked up her drink and swung around on the bar stool. She had to admit the club was up-market. The Spot stood on prime real estate in the centre of Sydney, drawing in its clientele from all the young up-and-comings that lived, partied and socialised in the inner city.

The Spot was tall, wide and solid stone, an old building with classic architecture of times gone by, and someone had had the brilliant idea of turning it into a trendy little club.

The music pumped out of speakers set well back in the room, wound up to a level that required a person to come within inches of another's ear to hear. If only the patrons weren't so big on sleazy pick-up lines…

A young man in a black jacket stopped beside Riana's stool and leant close. 'Do you believe in love at first sight? Or do I have to walk past you again?'

Riana opened her mouth, and closed it. He was just a boy, and the optimistic glint in his eyes struck her deep in the chest.

She tucked her dark hair behind her ears, stalling, trying to think of some easy let down. 'I do believe in love at first sight—' she paused, considering her words '—and I'm sure I'll know him when I see him…'

The boy raised his eyebrows. 'He's not me?'

Riana patted the young man on the shoulder lightly and offered him a conciliatory smile. 'I'm afraid not. Sorry.'

She sighed as the young man weaved his way through the crowd. She wasn't that much older than he was but she knew what she wanted. Tall, blond and hunky Stuart Brooks, of the Double Bay Brooks—a man that she knew right down to his slicked-back hair and suede jackets was the one for her.

Riana placed her empty glass on the bar.

'If I told you that you have a beautiful body would you hold it against me?' a deep, velvet-soft voice asked close to her.

Riana swallowed hard, a ripple of excitement coursing traitorously through her at the sensuality in his tone.

She shook herself. This was such a bad idea. She should put a sign up on herself saying 'taken'. She glanced at her left hand—it wouldn't be long now.

She turned, her breath catching in her throat. He was close, he was tall, and oh-so-cute.

His features were strong, almost chiselled. His hair short and chestnut brown, his eyes hazel with golden flecks, his jaw shadowed and his mouth all promises.

Her body warmed.

He leant closer. 'I'm waiting for your witty comeback.' And he smiled.

She lifted a finger, willing her brain to work, her senses spinning out of control at the sheer radiance of his smile, of the fire in his eyes, and of the mesmerising effect staring at his lips had on her.

He leant forward again, his spicy cologne invading her senses. 'You could just tell me to nick off, like the rest of them.' He threw a thumb in the direction of the crowd behind them.

Riana turned, surveying a bunch of guys gathered at a table in the far corner. Recognition slowly dawned. They were the one-line pick-up men that had propositioned her, one after another after another.

She expelled a breath, her mind clearing and her blood heating. 'What is it? Some game you guys are playing?'

Mr Golden Eyes shook his head, leaning close again to talk. 'No, it was Phil's last day with us at work—he had a better offer—and one of the boys gave him this book about dating.'

She frowned. 'And those terrible pick-up lines are in the book?' She had to laugh. 'And someone paid good money for it?'

He rubbed his neck. 'I have to be honest with you. The book says *not* to use them but we figured some of them didn't sound half bad. Besides, there are some real classics there.'

'Righty-o.' Riana frowned. 'How much have you guys been drinking?'

'*Touché*.' He smiled again, his golden eyes glinting. 'Okay, they may not be the best of lines but worth a try before we for ever scratch them from our repertoire.'

Riana leant in again to make herself heard over the music, and she couldn't help but breathe in his rich, spicy cologne. She wasn't sure whether to damn the music for being so loud, or to thank it. 'I can't imagine *you* using them.'

'Thanks.' His breath was warm on her neck. 'But you'd be surprised at how blank a mind can go when faced with a beautiful woman.'

She leant back. Was he saying *she* was beautiful?

Mr Golden Eyes leant an elbow on the bar and moved closer. 'So how am I doing?' he said close to her cheek.

How could he not think he was doing fine? He appeared to be everything a woman would want. Tall, dark, handsome, funny *and* intelligent. There had to be a catch somewhere…there always was.

'Talk fast,' she said to his neck, managing to keep a straight face. Let him sweat. Let him work to convince her why he was going to be different from all the rest.

'No more corny pick-up lines, I take it?'

She raised her eyebrows. 'I'll give you ten seconds. Nine…eight…seven.'

'You're the most beautiful woman here.'

Riana glanced at him, something strange fluttering in the pit of her belly. 'Flattering, but not good enough. Three…two…one.'

He widened his eyes, his eyebrows tilting to give him the most devastating puppy-eyed look she'd seen in her life. 'I just need to be loved, like everyone else does.'

Riana sucked in her breath and gave him a second look, past the handsome face, deep into his golden eyes where she saw an honesty that scared her.

He meant it.

That was what it was all about—looking for someone to share your life with, putting up with loud music, clubs and pubs, parties and people of all shapes and sizes to find the one meant for you.

She nodded, her pulse quickening. This guy was a crush waiting to happen on a girl's heart.

'That works,' she offered, trying to sound as calm and cool as she wanted to look. She could barely comprehend what she was doing. What about Stuart?

'Good, I'll tell the lads.' And his mouth curved into a smile.

Her stomach curled. What? Couldn't she at least have the satisfaction of telling him she was taken? That it was her that didn't want *him*? 'You don't want my number?' she blurted.

'No.'

'Oh? Not that I'd give it to you—' She raised her chin. What was wrong with her? What was wrong with him? Stringing girls along until they were all flustered...

He nodded. 'Sure.'

His disbelief was in his tone, as if no woman could refuse him! Riana crossed her arms over her chest. 'Do you get some sort of perverse pleasure in torturing women?' she asked, trying to keep her voice even. 'Chat them up and then leave them high and dry?'

He shook his head. 'Not usually, but in this case... I figured I'd even the score for the lads.'

She turned towards the men in the corner. She had been a bit short with some of them, a bit hard on others. She bit her bottom lip. He may have a point.

'Well done,' she said finally. 'But if you look at it from my point of view for a moment you may see that you lot owe me for putting up with being harassed.'

He leant closer, giving her another look, running his eyes down her body to her black leather boots, up her black trousers over her small metallic blue top to her lips and to her eyes.

Riana's body tingled as though he'd run his large hands over her, turning every nerve on as he went. She shifted on her stool.

'You're right,' he murmured. 'Let me buy you a drink for being such a good sport.' He gestured to the barman.

She smiled, satisfaction flowing through her at his concession.

'But you know, if a pretty woman like yourself doesn't want to get harassed by men you shouldn't sit at the bar alone.'

She lifted her chin, sobering. 'I'm waiting for a friend.'

'Male?'

She looked him in the eyes. Very presumptuous of him to ask, seeing as *he* didn't want her number. 'No. I'm waiting for my female colleague so I can meet a work contact.'

He nodded, not taking his eyes off her. 'Mixing pleasure with business?'

She shrugged. 'I guess.'

Mr Golden Eyes leant on the bar and surveyed the room. 'Me too. I have to meet some stuck-up designer who will probably waltz in wearing something screaming how good she thinks she is.'

Her breath caught in her throat.

He looked over her head. 'Who has the audacity to consider that I would turn my schedule upside down and inside out—'

She opened her mouth, a thousand retorts on the tip of her tongue. She took a
long, slow breath. 'Really, a designer?'
Riana asked slowly, leaning forward, her
pulse quickening. 'You wouldn't happen
to be a gifted but extremely arrogant photographer?'

His eyes widened a little. 'You?'

She held out her hand. 'Riana
Andrews—stuck-up designer.' She waved
a hand down her blue top and black trousers, trimmed with a silver belt, and large
silver hoops at her ears.

He didn't hesitate. 'Joe Henderson, foolish ass with foot in mouth disease.' He
stared her right in the eyes, taking her hand
firmly in his large warm one.

Sensation sizzled up her arm and ricocheted around her chest. Riana glanced
around for Maggie, still a no-show. 'I can't
say I'm thrilled to meet you like this,' she
stated dryly.

'Likewise.' Joe let go of her hand and slipped his hands into his pockets. 'You wouldn't hold this against me, would you?'

She raised her eyebrows. 'What? Your arrogant assumption or my beautiful body?'

He ran a hand through his hair and gave her a shrug, the corners of his mouth fighting a smile. 'Sorry about that.'

She tipped her head a little, eyeing him carefully. 'How sorry? Sorry enough to turn your schedule upside down to make amends for your big fat—'

'Possibly.' Joe nodded, rubbing his jaw. 'I hear you're quite a talent and are making a substantial mark on the world of wedding fashion.'

She stood up. 'I'm flattered at your late attempt at sweet-talk, but I assure you the only way you can make up for your terrible behaviour is to do my fashion shoot,' she said evenly, refusing to be intimidated by his sheer height, breadth and presence.

Joe stiffened.

Riana licked her lips. 'I know it's short notice and all, but you did agree to this meeting on the off-chance that you could accommodate me.'

Joe nodded slowly, running his hand over his rough jaw, eyeing her. 'I could probably manage it, seeing as you didn't come waltzing in here in one of your designer outfits.'

'That's big of you.' She looked across to the door. 'But did you consider for a moment that the last place I'd be flaunting my designs would be in a club like this?' She glared at the man. 'Seeing as they're bridal gowns and all.'

He shrugged, a soft smile tugging at his mouth. 'No one would have harassed you if you were wearing a wedding gown.'

She stared at him, her heart thundering in her chest. *This guy was different.*

'True.' She nodded, fighting a smile of her own. 'But then, you wouldn't have come up to me and I wouldn't now be waltzing out of here knowing how good I am.'

He crossed his arms over his chest, staring down at her. 'So I wasn't wrong? You are stuck-up and all?'

'I wouldn't want to ruin the mystery for you.' Riana smoothed down her outfit and stepped away from the bar. 'You'll have to wait and see.'

She forced her legs into action, determined to get away from the guy. She'd wait for Maggie outside in the fresh air and tell her of her success in securing Joe Henderson and his services.

She bit down on the end of her thumbnail. She wasn't so sure it was a good thing, though. That Joe wasn't crush material—he was a crash waiting to happen!

CHAPTER TWO

'SORRY I'm late.' Riana rushed into the fashion end of the bridal boutique that her family owned and ran. Nothing had gone right this morning. The power had gone out some time in the night so her alarm hadn't gone off, the hot water service had broken and she'd missed her train.

'Late?' Joe glared at her from a director's chair set up in the middle of the room, as though he was lord and master. 'You call this late? I call this a total disaster.'

'What?' Riana glanced around her. The room was filled with people, lights and camera equipment. A few of the men that milled around looked a lot like the guys who had accosted her with the bad pickup lines that night at the club.

21

She crossed her arms over her chest. The room was usually where the friends and family of the bridal party could audience a private showing, with the bride-to-be having her very own fashion parade. She'd decorated the place so it felt intimate and cosy. Today, it was wild.

'I said I was going to be here at eight a.m. sharp.' Joe narrowed his eyes, scrutinising her as though she had where she'd been written all over her. 'After all the trouble you went to to get me here I expected you to at least show some interest and have everyone ready to go.'

'Of course.' She sidled towards the heavy red curtains at the back of the room. 'And they will be.'

Joe's features darkened. 'It's after nine.'

She straightened tall. No way was she going to make excuses. She was his boss today and nothing he said could change that.

Sure, he'd caught her off-guard that time at the club, but not today. She'd keep distant, professional and absolutely cool when it came to Joe Henderson and his golden-flecked eyes and nicely built body.

She pulled her shoulders back. The lights were on, and there was no alcohol involved... There was no reason for her body to react to the guy at all.

Joe slipped off his seat and reduced the distance between them as though he were a charging bull. 'I need to talk to you.'

He stopped an arm's length away.

Her breath caught in her throat. 'Why?' She wet her lips and swallowed hard, trying to dispel the strange sensation in her belly.

He was cuter in the light than he'd been in the dimly lit club. Sure, his jaw was as shadowed as though he'd forsaken shaving in favour of the rugged look. And his blue jeans did hug his hips and long legs, driving home to every traitorous nerve in her body the perfection of his. And his chest—spread wide before her beneath a too-tight black T-shirt—screamed bad boy.

'How's it going?' Riana said calmly, meeting his brilliant eyes. 'I don't mean with the shoot—obviously, because you've just told me and I'm late. And not personally, because frankly I don't care what you're feeling personally.' She bit her tongue. She was babbling!

'Thanks.' Joe pursed his lips as though reconsidering something. 'I just wanted to say how sorry I am about that other night,' he stated dryly. 'It's been on my mind. I need to say that in no way did I want to hurt you by misleading you into thinking that I wanted a date with you.'

'Yes, you did.' She glared up at him. 'Evening the score I think you called it.'

Joe shrugged. 'You *were* hard on some of the lads.'

She stared up into his golden eyes, determined to get over whatever it was that being near him was doing to her body. 'It was no picnic for me.'

'I'm sorry.'

Riana stiffened. He sounded pretty sincere. 'Don't think for a moment that I wanted to go out with you.' She forced a laugh. 'I already have a wonderful man in my life.'

He crossed his arms over his wide chest. 'Really?'

She nodded. 'Absolutely.'

'Serious?'

What did he think? That she was devastated because he hadn't taken her number and needed his pity because she was oh-so-desperate? 'I have a date with him tonight actually.' She lifted her chin. 'It's at the romantic D'Amore and everyone knows that's where certain special announcements are made.'

He frowned. 'I have no idea what you're talking about.'

Typical. Only an absolute romantic-heathen wouldn't be aware that everyone who was anyone in Sydney got proposed to at the cosy little French restaurant. 'Stuart is going to propose to me tonight.'

'Oh.' He stiffened, his mouth thinning. 'And are you thinking of accepting?'

She smiled. 'Hell, yes. My two older sisters are happily married, you know.'

He tilted his head sideways, frowning. 'And that means…?'

Riana stared at the man. For someone purported to be savvy in business and getting quite a name in the industry for his expertise with the camera, he was absolutely hopeless. 'That it's my turn,' she said with emphasis.

'O-kay.' He rubbed his bristled jaw. 'I thought marriage was about love.'

Riana pressed her lips together tightly, holding the flood of retorts on the tip of her tongue. She let out her breath, crossing her arms over her chest. 'What's that supposed to mean? Just because *you* haven't got someone special in your life who loves you doesn't mean you can go and—'

He shrugged and turned away from her. 'Maybe you could get back there organised so I can stop sitting around and I can start doing my job.' And he strode away from her.

Riana gritted her teeth. As if she cared that she'd blurted out her most personal thoughts to a complete stranger and he'd walked away on her. Fine. Absolutely fine. He was the one who had stopped to chat in the first place... It wasn't as if it mattered who knew that Stuart was going to propose to her tonight. Tomorrow it would be in all the papers.

Riana slipped out the back, her chest tight. Maggie had assured her she wasn't needed at the six a.m. start the models would make to get organised with their make-up and hair, and she'd set out all the gowns days ago.

What had gone wrong?

The back room was in bedlam. Tall, lanky models stalked around, robes on, make-up and hair done to perfection.

Riana couldn't see there'd be a problem. The place was intact. The models all present and apparently accounted for. The gowns all hanging where she'd left them. 'Maggie?'

Maggie stuck her head out from one of the sewing rooms they were using as a changing-room. 'Thank goodness you're here. No one can agree who gets to wear what.'

'That's it? That's what all the fuss is about? For this I'm being harassed by Joe

Henderson and his inflated self-importance?'

Maggie shrugged sheepishly. 'He's the best in the business.'

'Which is why I'm going to put a great big smile on my face and not wrap my hands around his neck.' Riana grabbed the first lanky model and a gown off the rack. 'This, for you. Quickly.'

The woman dropped her robe and stepped into the gown. Riana adjusted the fit of the bodice, turned her around and laced up the back of the gown.

'Maggie, hand me the tiara with the medium veil.'

Riana took the tiara from Maggie and stood on tiptoe. She secured the tiara and veil to the woman's hair and gave her a gentle shove in the back. 'Right. Go.'

'He's a genius, that Joe, you know,' Maggie said, snaring another model by the arm and shoving her towards Riana. 'Have you seen his work?'

'Yes.' Riana took another gown off the rack. 'But the man's a monster. An arrogant self-absorbed, self-inflated—'

The model dropped her robe. 'Joe does demand a lot from everyone around him,' she said softly. 'But he's great, once you've got to know him.'

'That's good to know.' Riana zipped up the back of the dress and added a long veil, rolling her eyes at Maggie. The man probably knew every model on the continent, intimately.

'No truly, he helped out one of the young models who had got into drugs,' she said reverently. 'He's so nice. Always there for us all, you know.'

Riana stared at the tall, lithe blonde. She didn't want to hear how nice the guy was. She didn't care. She had Stuart, and Stuart was head over heels about her.

'He cares, that's all I'm saying, I guess.' The woman rotated slowly as Riana adjusted the fall of the skirts. 'Joe got her into rehab. And back with her family. They'd had a falling out over her modelling instead of going to university.'

'Thanks for sharing.' Riana managed a smile and pushed the model towards the front curtain. She didn't want to think about the guy a second more than necessary, especially how exactly all the models knew him so well. 'Next.'

'He is sort of cute in a rugged sort of way.' Maggie handed her a long, flowing veil.

She cringed. 'I've got Stuart.' And the last thing she needed was a crush on Joe, no matter what he made her body feel.

Maggie took a gown from the rack. 'Have you seen Stuart?'

Riana helped the next model into the gown, biting her lip. 'No, but he's so busy at work at the moment.'

Maggie zipped the gown up and fluffed up the flowing satin. 'Bummer.'

'Yes, I know. Just when I'm thinking that it's time we get more serious and spend more time together… But his work is very important.' Riana fixed the veil in place.

Maggie put her hands on her hips. 'He's an economist.'

Riana shrugged. 'Yes. Well, he takes the economy very seriously.'

'U-huh.'

Riana turned her attention to adjusting the fit of the strapless bodice of the satin gown. She knew Maggie's view of Stuart intimately. So, she didn't like him that much. It didn't matter. She wasn't going to be the one marrying him. Riana was. Mrs Riana Brooks had such a nice ring to it.

And she was sick of being alone, sick of the dating games, the bad kissers, the sleazy hands, the selfish needs of men out there, and of frozen dinners for one.

She was getting married. This year. She was sure of it. And Stuart Brooks was the man.

The D'Amore was all they said it was. From the time her oldest sister had announced her engagement, Riana had dreamt of this night.

Everyone knew the French restaurant was a place to take a girl to let her know how serious the relationship was. Her older sister, Tara, used it all the time for her proposal clients.

Riana shivered with anticipation and unabashed excitement. Stuart was seriously into *her*.

Would he push for a spring wedding? Would they honeymoon in Europe? Move in together in his apartment in the city or buy a house in the northern suburbs?

It was about time a guy fell totally in love with her. Wanted her to marry him. Live happily ever after.

Classical music drifted through the room. She couldn't help but smile as she sauntered into the bar, walking slowly, conscious of the impression Stuart would have of her when he saw her.

The kick-ass red dress she'd made for herself after her older sister's wedding clung to her curves, accentuating her shape, leaving no doubt that she was serious in her hunt for the perfect partner. The thin straps and plunging neckline gave the message of her simple elegance, and the thin necklace with a small golden heart spoke a thousand words as to what she wanted from him.

Stuart was at the bar, his hand gripped tightly around a double Scotch...or was it a triple?

'Honey?' She placed her hand on his shoulder and leaned over and kissed him. His breath was heavy with alcohol. How many drinks had he had?

'Riana, darling.' He glanced at his watch. 'You're late.'

'I'm always late.' She smiled.

He waved a finger at her, frowning. 'You know that I don't like it when I'm kept waiting.' He took her arm, his sober expression giving nothing away. 'Shall we eat then?'

She nodded. He didn't appear to be in the best of moods, but that could just be an act so she'd be more surprised when he popped the question. 'I hear the food here is wonderful,' she offered hopefully.

Stuart grunted and steered her to the entrance to the dining room.

The *maître d'* seated them near the back of the crowded restaurant. The table was small, draped with a pearl-white lace tablecloth with shining cutlery laid out, and a vase of roses nestled in the middle.

Stuart dropped into his seat, running his eyes over her body as she sank into her own seat. 'I have something important to ask you.'

Riana's breath caught in her throat. Already? She nodded, her heart pounding in her chest.

She could see it now. A beautiful apartment on the north side with views to the harbour, a man by her side sharing her life, a fluffy little dog and maybe, and in time, a child or three.

'Yes?' she whispered, leaning forward. Was he going to go down on one knee like in the movies? Was he packing a ring in his pocket? Did he have champagne organised as soon as she'd said yes?

He leant his elbows on to the table. 'I want you to go away with me.'

Riana looked into his face. 'Away?' Maybe he was taking the long way round to his proposal of undying love and intense need for her to be his for ever. Was it the honeymoon he was referring to?

'To Switzerland.' He lifted his hand for the waiter. 'My family has a chalet there and it's my turn to take advantage of it.'

Riana took a sip of water. 'How romantic,' she said with extreme calm, holding in her eagerness for the real question.

Did she have to wait long?

Switzerland had those beautiful mountains, with the snow-covered peaks, with the blue-blue skies overhead and a sprawling chalet just for the two of them... It would be a beautifully romantic place to have Stuart propose to her.

Stuart pulled out his cigarettes and tapped the box on the table as though he was itching to light up. 'Of course, we won't be alone exactly.'

Riana's body became heavy. 'Exactly?' she asked, raising an eyebrow at the man opposite her.

He waved a hand in the air dismissively. 'Well, there are a few friends I've asked to come to the chalet as well.'

Her body chilled. 'You've already asked them?'

Stuart waved a hand dismissively. 'Of course. I could hardly keep it to myself.'

But *she* was only just finding out? She swallowed hard. 'Sounds crowded.'

He shook his head and grinned at her. 'Not at all. We'll have a great time with my mates. And when I get tired of them—'

Riana stared at him, her mouth dry.

'You'll be there.' He took a gulp of the drink the waiter had put down in front of him. 'But I couldn't imagine being there without you. You're such fun to be with.'

'Fun?' she said dully. Was that all she was to him or was he just teasing her?

'Of course. You're a real blast to be with, Riana. Never a dull moment.' He leant closer, taking her hands in his. 'You're my little party animal... What's the matter?'

Riana looked at Stuart, her mind struggling to make sense of his words, while she tried not to. 'I thought...I thought we were moving to the next level...you know?'

She lifted her chin and glared at the man opposite her. This couldn't be happening to her.

Maybe it wasn't. Maybe she'd misheard, been mistaken. Stuart Brooks wasn't the sort of man who would toy with a woman. He had breeding, class and manners.

She shifted in her seat, determined. She wasn't going to go anywhere, least of all Switzerland, until she knew exactly where he figured this relationship was heading.

He furrowed his brow. 'Next level?'

'Yes,' she said softly, trying to smile at his act of naïvety. 'I thought you were going to propose to me tonight.'

Stuart closed his mouth tightly, making rumbling noises as though he was going to explode. 'Come on, you're kidding, right?' He laughed loudly.

'I thought you loved me?'

Stuart took a gulp of his drink. 'Do *you* love *me*?'

Riana placed her hand over her heart. 'I thought we had a future together.'

'Riana. Of course we do. A future of fun, sport, holidays…'

She opened her mouth, but the words wouldn't come.

Stuart sculled the contents of his glass. 'You're not exactly marriage material, are you?'

'Not marriage material!' She held her hands tightly on her lap, willing her legs to work, to get up, to get away, but she could barely breathe, let alone walk.

She was numb.

He wasn't serious about her. Not serious at all, and she'd just made a giant fool of herself, blurting out what she felt, yet again, to a man out to break her heart if she let him.

She stared at the man opposite her, watching his lips move, trying to take in his long-winded explanation over the rush of blood to her face and the heavy weight in her chest.

She choked back the burning sensation in her throat. She wasn't going to be Mrs Brooks. She wasn't going to be Mrs Anybody.

She wasn't ever going to find someone to love her, and the fact tore through her heart, ripping all her dreams to shreds.

CHAPTER THREE

JOE rearranged the tripod for the tenth time, standing back to assess the angles.

Thank goodness Tara Andrews had been around to let him in an hour ago. It had been late but she'd understood his need to get the equipment set up right for tomorrow. So much so that she'd left him to it, with exact instructions on how to lock up when he left.

Tara looked a lot like her sister, but had shorter hair, a far more cool and calm demeanour and a few years more experience in the world.

Joe rolled his shoulders, trying to dispel the tension. He wasn't sure what it was about today that sat uneasily in his chest. The lighting had been good. The models fantastic. The gowns awesome. Riana sure had a flair for the exquisite in her designs.

He looked through the lens. What was it that was off? Wrong? Off kilter? He couldn't put his finger on it...

He shook his head. Whatever it was he'd have to sort it out tonight for the re-shoot tomorrow. It was an absolute pain but he wanted to get it perfect for Riana.

'Marry me?'

Joe spun around at the woman's voice.

Riana stood in the doorway in a tight red dress that caressed her curves, accentuating how womanly she was. Her shoulder-length hair spilled around her shoulders like ebony waves, her lips pouty, her eyes wide and on him.

She leant heavily on the door-frame as though her legs weren't strong enough to hold her, a bottle dangling from one hand.

He frowned as the label became clear. Vodka. Half gone. What was going on?

'What—?'

She staggered forward. 'I said... Will you marry me?' she slurred.

He shook his head. He couldn't be hearing right. Or he was hallucinating. What was she doing here at this hour? Drunk? And proposing? He shook his head, trying to work her out. 'What—?'

She lifted the bottle and pointed it at him. 'Have you got a hearing problem?'

Joe slipped his hands into his pockets, eyeing her warily. This didn't feel like her at all. 'No,' he said carefully. 'No hearing problem.'

'Then?' She opened her eyes wide and waved her free hand in a circle as though she was rolling the tape faster.

She wanted to marry him? His blood heated. Did she like him? Was frustration behind her behaviour towards him today? 'Why on earth would you want to marry me?'

'Apart from your charming smile and scintilating wit...' She tried to smother a laugh, and failed. 'Because—' her voice broke '—because Stuart didn't propose at all. He didn't want me to marry him, he just wanted me to go to ski with him in the Alps...when he got bored with his friends.'

He cringed. The poor girl. She'd been so fired up earlier that the bloke was the one for her...

Riana shook her head, wiping her eyes with the back of her hand. 'He must have seen the look on my face.' She sighed heavily. 'And asked me what was up, so I told him...that I thought he was going to propose to me.'

Joe ran a hand through his hair. Hell. Talk about putting herself on the line. 'And?'

She took a gulp from the bottle, and gasped as the liquid slid down her throat, waving her free hand in front of her mouth as though the air would cool her mouth.

How was she drinking the stuff straight? If she was out to get herself blind drunk she certainly was on the way.

'And apparently he's *so* rich…his family has social standing…somewhere…and he made it abundantly clear that I wasn't…marriage material.'

Jeez, the guy was a total jerk. Wasn't it enough to break her heart? Did he have to drive what was left of her into the ground? 'So…' he offered cautiously.

She lifted her chin, took another swig from the bottle and swayed. 'So, I'm not his girlfriend any more.'

He stiffened.

She staggered forward, leaning against a chair. 'I'm the only one now who's a hopeless loser… I can't find anyone who wants to marry me.'

Joe ran a hand through his hair, his chest tight. This was the last place he'd expected to find he was needed. And she was the last person he expected to need him. 'Riana—'

She staggered across the room. 'I thought I'd be fending off the proposals by now.' She waved her arm around wildly. 'But…apparently…I'm all right for a bit of fun but not—'

Joe moved forward, his attention on all the cords, stands and equipment around the room. The last thing she needed was to be a damaged designer. 'Hey, there's nothing wrong with you.'

She brandished the bottle, staring at him, her dark eyes blazing. 'Yeah, right. Nothing. Then why am I alone again? Have you any idea how many boyfriends I've had?'

He shook his head. He could imagine. She was beautiful. Not the cover model sort of beautiful, but the smooth-skinned, bright-eyed, sweet-faced sort of beautiful that made your loins ache and your blood heat.

She stabbed the bottle of spirit towards him. 'I don't know either. I've lost count. It's so depressing, isn't it?'

He shrugged casually, inching closer to her, around the spotlights. He needed to make her safe, before something else happened to her. 'You weren't dumped *every time*?' he asked, more to make conversation than satisfy his curiosity. She couldn't have been. Who in their right mind would want to dump her?

'Course not,' she slurred. 'I dumped them *before* they could dump *me*.' She glanced around her. 'I can tell when they get that look in their eyes, when they're lying to me,' she whispered and lifted her chin defiantly. 'And there's no way I'd give *them* the satisfaction.'

She took another swallow from the bottle and swayed dangerously close to one of the tripods he'd set up earlier for his cameras.

Joe lunged forward and clasped her by the shoulders. She was softer than he'd imagined, her skin smooth and warm. Vulnerable.

Something primitive lurched inside him.

Joe shook off the sensation and propelled her over the cords to the carpeted steps of the platform, vividly aware of his hold on her.

He clenched his jaw tight and guided her down to a safe landing, trying not to think about how sweet she smelled, of strawberries and vodka. Of how warm the bare skin of her shoulders was, under his hands that itched to explore her. Or how beautiful her dusky eyes were, staring up at him with an open expectation that made his chest tight. What could he say? 'Steady on there.'

He straightened her up on the step. Her clients would probably strut their outfits here for their family and friends. All happy and full of hope. Nothing like Riana was now.

He sat down beside her as casually as he could manage. He had to get that bottle off her before she did something stupid. 'I could do with a drink myself,' he suggested lightly.

'Here.' She thrust the bottle at him and smiled. 'I like to share, and I'd make a good wife... I'm pretty sure.'

He took the bottle from her, ignoring the crazy lurch of excitement in the pit of his gut at her smile, at her warm body pressed beside his, of how close her full red lips were.

Joe took a swig, breathed through the liquid fire sliding down his throat and tucked the bottle behind his leg, out of view. 'Why marry *me*?'

'Why not?' She shrugged. 'I figure, what the hell... If I can't be anyone else's wife, I'll be yours.'

Joe stared at her. Words escaped him. Not the sort of flattery he was after. 'Right,' he managed. 'Okay.'

She leant towards him. 'You really want to know why?'

'Yes.'

'Cause if you won't have me,' she whispered, staring up into his face, her eyes glistening. 'No one will.'

His chest tightened. Hell. Was he that bad? How could she have got an impression like that about him? He shifted on the step, looking towards the door.

'Yep.' She nodded. 'You're rude, obnoxious and awfully scruffy...' She ran a hand down his coarse whiskers, shaking her head.

His blood rushed hot through his body, her fingers leaving a trail of burning desire down his jaw. What was she doing to him?

'I'm the bottom of the barrel?' Joe asked slowly. Surely all those years in university and then working his way into a reasonable reputation for finely executed photographs had counted for something?

She nodded earnestly. 'Yep. Bottom-bottom.'

Joe swallowed hard. 'And why do you feel that you need a man in your life, a husband, to feel complete?' he asked, cringing at his own idiocy. A bit of layman psychology wasn't going to be enough for this situation, not in a long shot.

She waved her hands in the air, tears brimming in her eyes. 'Everyone knows that life isn't the same if you don't share it.' She sagged against him as though the effort of talking had taken what was left of her energy, leaning her head on his shoulder. 'Where's the fun in doing stuff, movies, meals, places, if you don't share it?'

'True.' He had to agree on that one. Sure, he wasn't going looking for someone to marry but when you found the right person to fit comfortably into your life and share it with...

Riana straightened. 'So, will you share my life with me or will I have to go and find another bottle?' She stared at her empty hands then looked around her. 'Where's my vodka?'

'You don't need more booze. It won't solve anything.'

'Huh. Says you.' She dug around in the purse hanging off her shoulder as though she could find it in there.

Joe's gut tightened. 'You know the stuff can kill you?'

She shrugged, tipping her bag out, the contents spilling on to the floor. 'What the hell, like it matters...'

Joe stared at the scattered contents of her bag. She had enough make-up to start a small shop, plus a small can of hairspray, a couple of brushes, a mobile phone, loose change and receipts.

His gaze stopped on her car keys, memories of his sister flooding his mind. A tough break-up, booze, tears and car keys…

Raw grief sliced through him.

Hell, there was no way he could sit by and let Riana do this to herself—he looked her in the eyes—not when he could do something about it. 'Yes.'

She swayed towards him, her finely arched eyebrows lifting. 'What?'

He sucked in a deep breath. 'Yes.'

Her brow creased. 'Yes what?'

Joe cupped her face with his hands and stared into her beautiful dark eyes, praying that this would make all the difference to her. 'Yes, I will marry you.'

She smiled, her full red lips curving into a smile, her eyes brightening. 'You will?'

'Sure.' And as soon as she sobered up and came to her senses she'd dump him like she'd dumped every other man that came into her life. But at least she'd make it through the night without making a mistake that could cost her life.

She swung her arms around him and held him tightly. 'I'm so happy.'

Desire rippled through him. She felt *so* good. He tried not to breathe in her scent, take in the feel of her body pressed against his, or think about the wild responses deep within him.

She was all woman. Her alluring softness pressed against him. The sweetness of strawberries surrounded him. The soft scent of her shampoo invaded his senses as she held him close to her.

'I'm not a loser then, am I?' she whispered into his ear, her breath caressing the nerves in his neck, making promises that Joe knew could never be.

He shook his head, sucking in deep, slow breaths, bringing his arms up. He hesitated. Hell. He closed his arms around her, holding her close.

He couldn't have her think he didn't care about her. She had to believe that the proposal was real for now. That he loved holding her, loved the feel of her, the smell of her, the sweetness of her voice, no matter how slurred.

She had to see how much life she had yet to live.

Riana pulled back, running her soft fingertips down his bristly cheek, biting her bottom lip. 'Where's my ring?'

'Pardon?'

'You've got to give me a ring if we're engaged.' She smiled wildly at him.

Joe stared at her. Was she for real? She was amazing…unbelievable…drunk as hell…and such a romantic.

Hell. A ring. Where the hell was he going to get a ring from at this time of night?

He glanced at his fingers, all empty. Now would have been the perfect moment for that silver skull ring his mother had confiscated from him at sixteen.

Joe pulled the nearest camera bag over to him and flipped it open. Something he could use as a ring…? He undid one of the tripod legs and took the brass packer off the end. It looked about the right size.

He offered the small brass ring to her on his palm.

Riana pouted. 'Do it properly.' And she held out her hand as though she was in some old movie, awaiting a kiss from a handsome prince on her left hand. 'And you have to kneel.'

Joe ran a hand through his hair. 'Okay.' He tucked the vodka bottle into the camera bag and shoved it to one side. He dropped to the floor in front of her.

He looked up into her face, saw the tears brimming in her eyes. His gut tightened.

He swallowed hard and slipped the ring slowly onto her finger, his mind a mass of crazy thoughts, his body a frenzy of tangled urges. None of which he had any intention of pursuing.

'With this ring...' she murmured, listing to one side, a soft smile on her face, her eyes closed.

'That comes later,' he said, shaking his head. And in this case, not at all. He was already seriously involved.

She fell sideways.

Joe caught her in his arms, holding her. What a night.

He lifted Riana into his arms, sending a prayer to the ceiling that the morning would bring her some sense as well as sobriety.

The last thing he needed was another fiancée.

CHAPTER FOUR

Riana held her head and opened her eyes gingerly. Damn, what had she been drinking? She pried her tongue off the roof of her mouth and wet her dry lips, swallowing hard, trying to dispel the fur lining.

She was lying on the white sofa in her back office, her shoes on the floor, the spring silk samples draped over her like a blanket.

What was she doing here?

She vaguely recalled coming to the boutique last night...and before that? The wave of despair hit her. Stuart didn't want to marry her!

Her eyes burned. He was such a jerk. Using her like a plaything, something just for fun, to amuse him until someone worth getting serious over came along.

She stared at the ceiling. Why on earth wasn't she serious material? Sure, she may not have come from a rich family, or gone to a private school, but she had a class all of her own.

She shook her head. She was an idiot for even considering that he was worth her time, let alone her hand in marriage. The nerve of the man to tell her that she wasn't good enough for him or his high-and-mighty rich family!

She rolled off the sofa, holding her stomach with one hand, her head with the other, bracing herself against the pitching of her senses.

The floor wavered. Darn. She should have kept drinking so she didn't have to think about him, or feel like this.

She closed her eyes, resting on the edge of the sofa. At least she'd ended up safely here at Camelot Bridal Boutique and not in some gutter somewhere. That wouldn't have been a good look for a wannabe up-and-coming designer.

She cupped her cheeks, holding her face in the hope that it might still the vibrations gnawing at her head. She hoped she didn't look as bad as she felt.

She glanced at the clock on the wall. Seven-thirty. At least Joe couldn't complain this morning about her tardiness. Did she still have that change of clothes in her office from the last time she went straight from work to a club? She hoped so. She couldn't wait to see the look on Joe's face when he arrived and she was already here.

Joe…

She strained to think. There was something about him that she was missing. She shook her head tentatively. Whatever it was, it could wait. The last session with him was today and she wouldn't have to think about the scruffy-looking control freak again.

Riana stood up and staggered to the bathroom, her legs feeling as though all the alcohol she'd drunk last night had solidified there, every step jarring her brain and her stomach.

Waves of nausea slapped her senses.

Riana flicked the light switch in the bathroom and blinked away the pain behind her eyes.

She glanced at herself in the mirror. Mistake. Her hair was sticking out at wild angles as though something unspeakable had nested in it for the night. The smudges around her eyes from her make-up gave her the classic been-in-a-pub-brawl look, and her skin was as pasty as olive skin could get on a bad day. And, sheesh, it was a bad, bad day.

She turned the tap on. What she needed was a long hot shower to make her feel better, wash away all the comments Stuart had thrown around. Huh! She wasn't just for a good time.

She cupped her hands under the streaming warm water, her attention caught by the glimmer of gold on her hand.

What? A ring? On *that* finger?

Her belly lurched. She brought her hand up closer to her face. The small band looked like a wedding ring. She shook her head as much as her aching brain allowed. But it couldn't be. Whirlwind weddings didn't happen in Australia. There were no Vegas altars available twenty-four-seven here.

Riana knew this for a fact. Her older sister, Skye, was forever being asked how fast a wedding could take place—mostly by young couples too caught up in the amazing raptures of love to think straight.

It was a month, she was sure of it. And it could only be less if someone was dying—if she was remembering right. She did have the habit of blocking out her sisters' talk about work.

She fingered the band. *Who?*

Had she done it herself, knowing she deserved to be as happily married as her sisters? Or had someone else put it there? *Why?*

She scrunched her eyes tightly closed, clawing for any hint of last night's desolation and subsequent commiseration with a bottle of vodka.

Joe's face came to mind.

Riana grabbed the sink for support. Something to do with Joe Henderson, photographer extraordinaire, last night?

She could remember his face, strong and angular, his jaw rough with bristle. She closed her palm, almost feeling the sensation on her fingertips.

She'd touched him?

Flashes came to mind. Of kind words, his velvet-smooth deep voice, his golden eyes looking down at her with a warmth that made her toes curl.

What had she said to him? Her throat burned. The last thing she wanted was that man to know all her woes, especially after bragging up Stuart's imminent proposal.

She sagged to the floor. Could she have acted more like an idiot if she'd tried? Fancy believing in the jerk so much that she'd told everyone that he was going to propose, including Joe.

Tears burned her eyes and made her throat ache with the need to yell. She was a fool.

Memories flooded her mind—of all the time she'd taken to spend with Stuart, of all the energy she'd spent on him, all the smiles, the flirting, the amazing outfits. And he was just like every other jerk that she'd met.

She stared at the ceiling, futilely blinking back the tears. She'd even told her mother she could stop worrying about her, that she was going to settle down too, like her sisters.

She let the tears flow, let the sobs rack her body, cursing her big fat mouth. Everyone was going to know now how much of an idiot she'd been with Stuart. He hadn't loved her at all.

There was a light tap on the door.

'Hey?' said a deeply male voice. 'Are you okay in there?'

Riana staggered to her feet, choking back the tears and the pain in her head. Couldn't a girl have a quiet cry on her own bathroom floor without being interrupted? She flung the door open. 'What?' she snapped.

Joe Henderson stood in front of her, freshly shaved, his hair combed back, his blue jeans fitting very nicely on his body, and his white T-shirt stretched tightly across his wide chest.

Riana looked up into his golden-flecked eyes. They were wide with concern, looking at her as though she was a fragile butterfly who'd head-butted a wall.

'Are you okay?'

She straightened taller, trying not to cringe at the splitting ache in her head at the slightest movement. She didn't need his pity. 'I'm fine.'

He lifted an eyebrow.

She swiped at her damp cheeks with the back of her hand. Darn. Now she must really look bad after turning on the waterworks. She was probably all blotchy. 'You're being nice,' she accused.

He slipped his hands into his pockets. 'Well, yes. After last night...'

Last night? She clasped her hands tightly in front of her, tilting her head and probing his eyes for what in heavens she'd said or done last night. 'I wanted to talk to you about last night.'

He nodded. 'I figured you would.'

She looked at her feet. *What had she done with him?* Her body tingled and heat shot to her cheeks. No. She couldn't have done *that*. Not with him. No.

Riana let her gaze wander up Joe's very long legs, over his flat stomach, up his solid chest, ignoring the urge to run her hands up along his muscles, to his smooth face and soft, warm eyes.

Her body heated in places she didn't want to think about. She bit her bottom lip. She couldn't have, could she?

She stared into the man's face, giving him a second look. He certainly wasn't acting the same man as yesterday. Something big had to have happened between them to cause such a change in him.

Realisation dawned. Her body's reactions to him were evidence enough, let alone his turn-around in mood towards her. She must have made love to him!

'Oh, no. No.' She covered her face. 'I'm going to just die.' She swung away from him, her cheeks blazing, her stomach tight and her head throbbing.

'Hey,' he said softly, laying his large hands on her shoulders and turning her round.

A shiver raced down her spine at his warm hands against her bare skin. Darn. She wished she could remember what her body obviously did. She would have thought that of all the things she would have remembered it would have been making love to Joe Golden Eyes.

'It's not as bad as you think.'

Rushing from one disaster into the arms of another? Yes, it was. It so totally was.

'Hey?'

'No,' she whispered. 'No. It's worse.' How could she look him in the face? What sort of woman made love to a stranger while she was drunk? A fool. A total fool.

'Nothing is as bad as it first appears.' He patted her shoulders. 'Trust me.'

'Oh, really?' She swallowed hard, her mind a throbbing mass of tangled thoughts. How could she have slept with the photographer from hell? Why was she so hopeless when it came to men? 'Tell me then why I shouldn't just go and kill myself?'

He lifted her chin and stared down into her eyes, his brow furrowed. 'You have a lot to live for.'

Riana could just imagine the looks on her sisters' faces when they heard about her latest act of madness. As if she didn't have enough on her mind with Stuart's defection from a committed relationship.

'You have me,' he said softly. 'I'll be here by your side.'

She jerked her chin up. 'You?' She didn't pick him as the sort of guy to stick around after he'd notched up another conquest on his bed-head.

'Sure.' He pushed a wisp of hair from her face, diplomatically avoiding staring at the wild mess on her head. 'I meant it last night when I said I wanted to marry you.'

His words struck her like a wrecking ball to the chest. 'Marry me?' she whispered.

He smiled down at her, his eyes bright and warm and caring. 'Sure, you're a wonderful, beautiful woman who has everything to live for.'

'Live for?' she echoed, her heart pounding in her chest a million miles an hour. What was he talking about? Marriage? This couldn't be happening, couldn't be real.

'Sure,' he said softly. 'There must be a million things you can be doing rather than dwelling on the past, like designing your wedding dress.'

'Wedding dress…' Riana lifted her hand and stared at the brass band on her finger, vaguely recalling Joe's face and some words…*With this ring?*

He stroked the brass band. 'Don't worry, we'll get something better than this for you later on. It's all I had on me at the time,' he said steadily, watching her closely as though to gauge her response to his words. 'Don't worry about anything.'

Riana stared at the man in front of her, her body as numb as her mind. So she hadn't made love to him, but what in heavens *had* she done?

He glanced at the office door. 'I've got to get going—everyone's arriving. Just take your time, your assistants are with the models. No need to rush.' He leant forward and brushed his lips over her forehead. 'I'll see you later, okay?'

'Okay,' she breathed, her skin burning where his kiss had touched her.

She wasn't numb any more, she was on fire…and engaged to a stranger!

Joe ran his hands through his hair, striding out of Riana's back office and into the throng of models and seamstresses. Hell. He'd thought the morning would have brought Riana some perspective on the situation. It hadn't. She seemed as upset and distraught as she had been last night over the break-up.

His gut wrenched anew at the echo of her sobs, of her wide-eyed stare, of her voice tight with pain, and of her tear-streaked face.

He clenched his fists by his sides. She must have really loved the guy. Like his sister had loved a guy, and lost him, and herself.

He stalked down the hallway, past two of Riana's assistants dressing one of the models. Yesterday had made a big difference to them all. Frozen in indecision at the beginning of proceedings the day before, they were relaxed and confident today.

Joe strode into the front room and went to his cameras. He picked up the nearest, holding it close.

His chest tightened, the haunting memories of his sister's last days bombarding him.

Hayley had been about the same age as Riana when she'd fallen in love. As full as life. As optimistic and energetic, and as keen to have someone to love her for ever.

He hooked the camera over his neck, trying to dispel the harsh claws of his memories. 'Okay, folks, let's get this show on the road.'

If only he'd seen his younger sister's distress over her boyfriend dumping her as serious. He'd brushed it off, giving her only the most cursory of consolations, a quick hug, a joke and what he had thought was a pep talk for the future. He couldn't have imagined she'd have no future.

She'd been dumped before—it hadn't been the first time. If only he'd realised that those times were different.

Joe looked through his camera. 'More light. I need more light,' he barked, his voice heavy with the weight of his guilt.

His little sister had hidden herself away in her place after he'd flown out, apparently drinking and smoking, sinking into a deep despair.

If he'd known he would have done something. Anything, to shake her out of her tunnel vision of misery, but he'd been in Bali covering a bathing suit spread, furthering his career, which at the time had seemed far more pressing than holding his sister's hand through her break-up.

'Let's get this moving,' he yelled, training his camera on the curtains. He snapped the tall blonde as she came through the curtain, radiant in a shimmering white satin gown trimmed with lace and studded with pearls that caught the lights.

'It's your wedding day,' he barked at the girl. 'Smile like it is. Smile knowing you're going to marry the man you love and he loves you.'

Hayley hadn't been able to see past that bloke not wanting her. Certain he had been the only man that she could ever love. And he hadn't loved her.

'Work it.' Joe snapped again and again, staring at the girl in her wedding gown through the lens. She was good. He could almost believe she was going to marry someone today.

It was all Hayley had dreamt of. Her and that bloke. The police had figured she had been on her way to his place when it had happened.

She'd got in her car half plastered and had driven until the tears had blinded her to the oncoming traffic, to the bend in the road, to the tree that ultimately took her life.

Joe gripped the camera tighter. He wasn't going to watch another young woman do the same thing to her life. He was going to help Riana through this.

He was going to give her something to hang on to until sanity prevailed...until sense overrode the despair...until she wasn't blinded by her loss or her broken heart any more.

'Great.' He managed to smile. 'Turn, slowly.' He'd save Riana from herself.

There was no way that he was going to make the same mistake again.

CHAPTER FIVE

RIANA untied the intricate laces on the last dress and helped the tall, dark-haired beauty to climb out of it. 'Thank you. You did wonderfully.'

She watched the model move away with an ease and a calm that Riana envied. After hours in the vicinity of Joe Henderson she still looked as fresh as first thing in the morning. Riana, however, was fraying at the edges just thinking about him.

She'd just managed to keep herself in one piece for the last five hours. Her head was splitting in two. The confusion about last night didn't help, but she'd soldiered on regardless.

She'd drunk a gallon of water in the hope of flushing out her system and her hangover, but that had only meant she was in the bathroom more than ever, staring at her doleful pasty face and cringing over her stupidity.

Had this morning really happened with Joe? She couldn't tell… She could've been dreaming for all she knew. There was no way at the moment she could discern where dreams ended and reality began.

Riana slipped the gown on to a hanger, tying the back of the bodice up again. Last night would have made for a weird dream, even weirder if it ended up to be real.

She had to be delusional. Things like instant proposals didn't happen between strangers…surely?

She glanced at the band on her finger. Still there.

Riana closed her eyes and sighed. The only way she was going to find out the truth about last night, and soon, was to confront Joe, knowing she was awake, relatively sober, and sane.

She looped the train of the dress on to the next hanger, folding the fabric carefully so it sat evenly. How to ask the question? It was embarrassing no matter which way she thought of it. If what had happened this morning was just a dream, her asking would show him that she'd been fantasising about him asking her to marry him, touching her, touching him.

If it was real… She shook her head. It was probably another gag he and his mates were perpetrating on her, for some unfathomable reason.

She straightened tall. She couldn't put off facing the guy and getting down to the bare bones of last night's events.

She bent over, kicking off her shoes, her feet almost as sore as her head. A wave of nausea hit her, bile rising in her throat, making her eyes burn.

She sagged against the wall. She'd have to eat soon before her stomach stuck to her spine.

'You okay?' Joe's warm voice was right beside her, his hand skimming across her back and around her waist, taking her weight.

She nodded, fighting the bolts of tingling sensation his touch caused in her.

'Liar.' He helped her to the nearest seat. 'Have you eaten? You look like hell.'

She managed a smile. 'Thanks. I feel it. And no, I haven't eaten.' She'd barely had time to breathe trying to keep up with the shoot, the wardrobe changes, and the alterations to a last minute gown that just didn't want to go right.

'How about we get lunch together?' he offered, his voice deep and velvet-soft. 'We could talk.'

She nodded. 'We need to.'

He stood up. 'Give me fifteen minutes to finish up here, okay?' He started down the hall. 'The shoot went great.' He twisted slightly, shooting her a grin. 'You're going to be a sensation and a half.'

Riana nodded again, not trusting her voice, the warm glow spreading through her chest and radiating out to her extremities. Why would a compliment from him make her feel so...good?

'What was that about?' Maggie came up beside her. 'Were *you* just being nice to him?'

Riana watched Joe's stride, his presence commanding as he moved through the hall, issuing orders to his crew about how he wanted the set packed up, and quickly.

'What's going on? Come on,' Maggie begged. 'I've been stuck in the office with the phones going non-stop. I've missed out on everything. Why do you look like hell?'

Riana opened her mouth, but what could she say?

'And why are you wearing that trouser suit that's been sitting in your office for the last two weeks? What's he doing being nice to you and vice-versa? Tell all!'

Riana smoothed down the black trousers, concentrating on picking off the specks of fluff that she must have picked up during the morning. Could she tell Maggie what she thought had happened, or would it all vanish, dissolve like a dream?

She sucked in a deep breath. She was her *best* friend and telling someone might make it seem real. 'You wouldn't believe what I think I went and did. Last night—'

Maggie grinned. 'You said yes to Stuart and you're going to have a spring wedding.'

'No. No.' She waved a hand dismissively, shaking her head. Stuart was so over.

'But it looks like I *am* going to be married.'

Maggie pushed her blonde hair back off her shoulder, pursing her lips. 'That's what I said.'

Riana shook her head. 'Not to Stuart.'

Her friend frowned. 'To who?'

'Joe.'

'The photographer Joe? You have to be kidding? You two hate each other's guts, don't you?'

Riana shrugged. 'I thought I did.'

Maggie drew a chair over to Riana's and dropped into the seat, leaning close to her. 'What happened?'

Riana drew a slow, deep breath. 'I think he proposed to me and I said yes,' she blurted in a rush. Could it really be true? Finally, someone wanting to marry her, love her, keep her safe, give her everything she always wanted.

Maggie stared at her, her mouth open as if words failed her. 'When?' she finally said. 'How?'

'Last night.'

Her friend frowned. 'But you were with Stuart last night, weren't you?'

'He didn't want me. He just wanted some fun.' She shrugged, trying not to succumb to the tearing ache in her chest at her sheer stupidity for believing he could ever be the one she'd settle on. 'He didn't think I was serious relationship material.'

Maggie let out a breath. 'And he told you that?'

Riana stared at the wall opposite them, her cheeks heating. 'After I pushed him a little.'

'You have a tendency to do that.'

Riana swung to face her friend. 'Well, how else am I going to find out what a guy's thinking?'

'Be patient like the rest of us.'

'That's not me. You know that's not me. I can't wait around without knowing.' Riana shook her head. 'So I dumped him, bought a bottle of vodka and walked here.'

'No.' Maggie sat back and stared at her. 'From D'Amore? That's like five kilometres?'

Riana nodded, flexing her toes on her aching feet, the reason for her discomfort dawning on her. 'I think I must have been out of it by the time I got here because I don't remember much. I'm not even sure whether it happened.'

Maggie leant closer. 'Do you remember him proposing?' she whispered, looking around at the models packing up their stuff.

Riana shrugged. 'Sort of. I remember the ring.' And those words ringing through her head like an echo. *With this ring.*

'He had a ring for you?'

Riana thrust her hand towards her friend, showing her the shiny brass band on her ring finger. 'He said he'd get me a proper one later.' And the thought made her all warm inside. He had not only proposed to her on the spur of the moment, he'd found a ring for her and given a promise of another, bigger, better, brighter one.

Maggie shook her head. 'This is weird.'

'I know.' Riana nodded. 'Could it be real?'

'Have you talked to him about it?'

Riana stood up slowly, vividly aware of the minutes flying by until she'd be with Joe Henderson again, out with him, talking with him about last night.

Was he going to say how much he wanted her? Loved her? Her belly tightened. 'I tried this morning, but he's so nice and gentle and so into me and…and…'

'And what?'

'He kissed me.' She touched her forehead, caressing the spot on her forehead with her fingertips, smiling softly as an echo of the wonderful sensation he had caused in her raced through her body. 'It was so…beautiful.'

'Oh…my…God. You have it bad for him!' Maggie laughed, leaning backwards, her eyes bright and wide.

Riana sobered. 'Of course not. I'm not sure I even like the man. And I don't even know him… I just met him, you know.' She shrugged, looking away. There was no way she'd get *that* caught up in a guy. Ever. 'And there's no guarantee that last night even happened. It could have all been a dream.'

'No, it couldn't. There'd be no way you would have dreamt *that*.' Maggie grinned up at her. 'But you're hot for him.'

Riana shook her head, lurched to her feet and strode down the back hallway. 'Am not.'

'It's written all over your face,' Maggie said from behind her.

Riana pushed open her office door. There was no way she'd fall for Joe. 'You're not helping.'

Maggie came up behind her. 'What am I meant to say? A man proposes to you out of the blue...and, let me remind you, a man that you would *normally* give a flat out no to. So, obviously, in your drunken state your subconscious was doing the thinking for you. So, maybe you're meant to be with him? Maybe you're soul mates and he saw it on the spot.'

Riana swung to face Maggie, a thousand refusals on her tongue. 'But the things he's said to me?'

'The banter of a shy man unable to truly express himself,' she offered. 'Maybe.'

Riana eyed her friend warily. Joe shy? 'If he was so shy then last night shouldn't have happened—'

'Of course it could have happened. It did. He probably felt more comfortable with you being so loose and easy, and happy, and far less acerbic than you usually are with strange cute men.'

'You're talking nonsense.'

'Then call it off,' Maggie said, waving a hand in the air. 'Tell him no. Tell him you don't want to marry him.'

'I might.' She chewed on her bottom lip. But maybe Maggie was right, maybe she should trust her subconscious with a man for once. She certainly hadn't done well so far on her own. And if he liked her that much, then who was she to argue?

That was half her trouble…trying to find a man who loved her, who wanted her so much that he wanted to share his life with her. And here he was.

She fiddled with the brass band on her finger, savouring the glimpse of a memory from last night, of Joe on his knees in front of her, sliding the ring on to her finger. *With this ring.*

She sighed. Being married to a cute, shy photographer might just be what she had always wanted.

He could be all her dreams come true…

CHAPTER SIX

RIANA smoothed down her dark hair, arranging it on her shoulders, this way, then that way, then ruffling it. She had no idea whether it was just to do something to pass the time or to look good for Joe.

She paced the front office in front of Maggie's desk, smoothing her trousers down again. It was a dull outfit for a designer to go out in. Joe probably expected her to wear something loud, with bold colours and darts, tucks and a heap of lace or crazy hemlines.

She darted a look at her friend, biting her lip. 'I'm not typical designer material. If he's expecting some outgoing, party-animal—'

'Then he's got the right girl.' Maggie looked up from her computer. 'You are outgoing. You love parties and you do wear your own designs when you go out somewhere very flash and special—they're just more traditional and elegant. You're a wedding gown designer, remember?' Maggie shot her a smile. 'And it's only lunch.'

She nodded. Maggie was right. Just lunch. With Joe.

Riana ran her fingers through her hair. 'This is weird,' she murmured, glancing up the hallway again. Could it really be happening? Could she be engaged? Could Joe Henderson really have fallen so totally in love with her at first sight, that night at the club, that he would propose to her on the spur of the moment like that?

She swung to Maggie. 'Can you come too?'

Maggie shook her head. 'This is something you have to work out on your own. Me holding your hand won't help.'

Riana smoothed down her hair. 'Please.'

'I don't know what's up with you,' Maggie quipped. 'You don't usually get nervous about men.'

She straightened. Maggie was right, but Joe Henderson wasn't just any man. He stirred things in her that she hadn't let any man stir in her.

'Riana,' said a deep male voice behind her.

She turned. Her name on Joe's lips did something strange to her belly. 'Hi,' she managed.

'Ready?' His gaze raked her, his eyes moving boldly from her black stilettos, up her trousers, over her shirt to her face as though it was the first time he was seeing her today.

She nodded.

His eyes bored into hers with an intensity that almost scared her, but it was just lunch. Nothing more. She was in total control here, of herself and her emotions, and if what Maggie had said was right, of Joe too. She had nothing to worry about.

She reached for her bag, her blood raging through her ears like a torrential flood. The bag fell to the floor, the contents scattering across the room.

She covered her mouth to smother her expletive, her cheeks heating. Oh, she was such an idiot.

Riana dropped to her knees, bowing her head to hide her face. What would he be thinking of her now? If there was any way to show him how clumsy and inept she was in the shortest amount of time, she had to find it.

She couldn't look at him.

'Let me help,' Joe offered, his voice deep and soft, squatting down beside her and picking up her scattered make-up, her hairbrush, her car keys...

She swept up her compact, her breath mints, the rest of her make-up and her perfume and shoved them back into the bag, unable to raise her eyes to his. The first guy that she'd met who believed in love at first sight and she was out to show him how blind he was.

She opened her bag, holding it out to him, her eyes down, waiting for him to drop his load into her bag, her heart pounding in her chest like a stampede of elephants.

He held her things over the bag, pausing.

Riana bit her lip.

Joe placed his load into the bag reverently as though he knew how much all her things meant to her.

She swallowed hard, closing the bag.

Joe touched her chin gently with his forefinger, lifting her chin. 'Hey?'

She met his brilliant golden-flecked eyes. 'I'm sorry,' she blurted. She'd never been with someone who really loved her before.

Joe took her hand and stood up, drawing her up with him. 'You've got nothing at all to be sorry about.'

'I'm such a klutz.'

He shook his head. 'You're probably still a bit hung-over, that's all,' he offered, staring down into her face.

She hadn't thought of that. She nodded. 'Yes. I should avoid driving or operating heavy machinery.'

'Absolutely.' Joe grinned. 'Hungry?'

'Starving.' She looked back at Maggie, who shot her a thumbs-up and a mischievous grin.

If Riana didn't know better she'd say that Maggie had been shooting arrows from Cupid's bow while he wasn't looking. She only hoped she'd got the right guy—she didn't need another disaster.

The café on the corner, a block from the boutique, was the perfect location to take Riana for lunch. More because he'd found it yesterday and it wasn't far to go, than for the ambience or cuisine. Joe figured the simpler he kept things, the better.

The silence that had descended between them after they'd left the boutique was heavy. Joe didn't know quite what to say. He couldn't pick up what she was feeling.

After that bag episode in reception it was clear to him that she was easily upset by small things. He'd have to tread carefully, watch her carefully, read her carefully for the right moment to tell her the truth. But only when she was ready. Totally ready.

Her boyfriend had been an idiot to brush her aside like he had. She was beautiful, talented and put a damned brave face on for everyone around her.

If he didn't know exactly what had happened, seen how hard she'd taken it, heard her grave comments, seen her despair, he wouldn't have picked her as a woman with a broken heart. Not when she was so competent at work, brave in front of her staff, acting almost normally.

It was the glimpses that frightened him.

Memories of his sister and what she must have gone through in that last week of her life haunted him. He should have been there. He shouldn't have gone away. If only he'd known—realised how serious a broken heart could be.

He would give anything to do it again. Steal time and go back and make it right. He knew it was impossible, but helping Riana wasn't.

'It's a nice place,' he murmured as they entered the small café, more to get her to talk than anything. 'You probably come here often?'

'Yes,' she said softly.

What she was thinking he had no idea. Could a woman with a broken heart function normally? He would have thought she'd have come round by now and called the engagement off. But then, his sister's grief had consumed her for an entire week before—

Riana walked in front of him, her hips swaying gently as she moved between the tables, most occupied, to the ones at the front near the window. 'The food is good here.'

He followed, his hands clenched by his sides, trying to keep his eyes off her curves and on the task at hand—looking after her.

Joe pulled back his shoulders and walked taller, watching the perfect shape of her butt in those dark trousers, running his eyes down her long legs, wondering what they'd feel like wrapped around him.

He shook himself. This was probably the craziest thing he'd ever done. He liked helping people out. He just hadn't gone to this extreme before... But then, this time was special. For Hayley as much as for Riana.

Joe caught Riana's elbow and propelled her past the window tables to the back corner of the room to ensure their privacy. The last thing he needed was someone who knew about him and his fiancé Francine to drive by and see him with a beautiful woman.

Joe moved in front of her and held her seat out, his eyes falling on how her silky black hair fell around her shoulders, and how sweet she smelled, like strawberries and vanilla.

She sat down slowly.

It was all he could do not to lean over her and kiss the top of her head, her ear, her cheek, her throat, and those rich dark lips of hers.

He forced his legs to move to his seat. He dropped into it, clenching his jaw against his inappropriate urges. 'So, I guess now would be a good time to—'

She looked at him with her dark eyes, bright with purpose. She looked so hopeful that he couldn't bear to hint at the truth. He'd have to be sure when he did that she was okay. The worst thing he could possibly do would be to be another blow to her.

'To find out all about you,' he blurted, watching her carefully.

'Yes.' She laid a napkin in her lap. 'That would probably be a good idea, considering.'

Joe picked up the menu off the table and stared at it, her sweet voice sliding over him like a hundred kisses. He swallowed hard. 'So?'

Riana laid her hands on the menu in front of her on the table. 'Tell me…do you have brothers? Sisters?'

He shook his head. He couldn't afford for her to find out too much about him. Besides, it was probably better that he focused on how much she had in her life to hang on to, how much she could be grateful for. 'You first. I know your whole family is a part of Camelot—'

'Not all.'

He couldn't help but notice the dark shadow that passed over her face. He leant forward, fighting the insane urge to hold her in his arms.

She looked towards the front door of the café. 'My father left us when I was eight.'

'I'm sorry.'

She shrugged, clenching her hands tightly. 'It was a long time ago. It doesn't matter.'

Right. He eyed her carefully. Sure it didn't. He certainly wasn't going to mention her father again. 'So your mother and you and—?'

Riana's mood seemed to lighten instantly. 'My oldest sister is a part-time wedding planner who does proposal planning the rest of the time.'

'That's different,' Joe said, considering it. He couldn't imagine getting help to propose to a woman, but then, he guessed there were men out there too shy to feel comfortable just doing it.

'Yes, but it's catching on.' Riana almost smiled. 'A lot of men these days are too busy or too romantically challenged to give the time a proposal deserves.'

He nodded. 'We didn't have any trouble on that front.'

'No.' She blushed.

Joe couldn't help but smile. He would have to say that never in his life had he been proposed to. And take out the fact that she didn't like him and she'd assured him that he was the bottom of the barrel, it would have been sweet. More than sweet, wonderful.

A tall thin woman stopped beside their table, a pen and pad in hand. 'Can I take your order?'

Joe glanced at the menu. 'Sure. Club sandwich and a black coffee.' He looked at Riana staring at the menu dully as though she barely saw it, let alone had any interest in food at all. He'd have to make sure she looked after herself.

They'd said his sister had replaced food with alcohol.

Joe scanned the other patrons' meals. 'The chicken roll looks good,' he offered.

She looked up, startled, and nodded. 'Yes. I'll have the chicken roll.'

'And the orange juice looks like it's freshly squeezed,' he prompted, glancing at the next table as though he could see it instead of the glass of cola. No way did Riana need a caffeine hit just now.

Riana nodded. 'Orange juice would be nice.'

The woman nodded and left.

'Thanks,' Riana said softly.

Joe shrugged. 'You didn't look into it.'

She glanced at him with wide eyes as though he'd read her thoughts. She shrugged, sobering. 'I have other things on my mind.'

His gut tightened. Like that Stuart and how her life would have been if he'd reciprocated her feelings and wanted to spend his life with her.

'You were telling me about your family business,' he stated casually. The last thing she needed to dwell on was that jerk who'd dumped her.

She brightened. 'My other sister, Skye, is a wedding planner proper and so is my mother. Skye is training Maggie part time to be her assistant.'

'You went a different way then.' Joe leant back as the waitress came back quickly to put down their orders.

She nodded. 'Yes.'

Joe spun his plate around, surveying the fresh bread and the aromatic filling. 'Piping to your own beat.'

She nodded. 'Something like that.'

'You have a lot of talent,' he enthused. She had to see that there was more to life than Stuart. 'You could be very successful with contemporary fashion.'

Riana shrugged. 'I like wedding gowns.'

'It shows.'

'Thanks,' she said softly, a smile tugging at the corners of her full lips.

He couldn't tear his gaze from her lips. Full, blood red, enticing. His body heated.

'I really feel like a fairy godmother who's dressing Cinderellas in all shapes and sizes.' She closed her eyes, a soft smile playing on her lips. 'For their princes…and their magical balls.'

Joe stared at her. She was beautiful. 'Your mother's still single?' he managed, clenching his fists under the table. What was she doing to him? How? She was just another woman he was helping.

'Yes, but not for want of trying. Since Tara and Skye got married she started going out again.' She picked up a stray piece of lettuce off her plate and put it in her mouth. 'There's this certain gentleman that she really likes—'

Joe stiffened. It sounded as if it had taken her mother a long time to get over her father. He hoped Riana wouldn't take that long getting over that Stuart creep— they'd be married with five kids. The implication sent a warmth coursing through him.

'I have to ask.' Riana stared at the meal in front of her, picking at the chicken sticking out from the edges of her roll. 'Do you really want to marry me, Joe?'

'Sure.' He didn't hesitate. He reached forward and took her hand in his, running his thumb in small circles on her palm, delighting in the amazing softness and fragility. 'Do *you* still want to marry me?'

He pressed his lips together tightly. This was it. This was his out if there was any doubt at all in her mind. If there was a chance that sanity had surfaced over her grief and despair. If she'd decided bottom of the barrel wasn't good enough for her any more.

Joe's gaze was drawn to her face. Her wide dark eyes were searching his with a wild purpose. His gut knotted. 'I just want you to be happy,' he blurted. He had to ensure that she wouldn't just call it off out of low self-esteem.

Her eyes glistened. 'That's really sweet, you know?' she whispered, her voice thick and husky. 'No man has ever said that to me before.'

Her words twisted around his heart. He dragged in a deep breath and gave her hand a gentle squeeze. 'You mustn't have known many nice men.'

'No. My track record has been pretty bad.' She leant over the small table and pressed her hot lips against his cheek. 'Thanks for being so wonderful.'

Joe nodded, and glanced down at his sandwich, fighting the surge of blood rushing to his loins. Fighting the urge to touch his cheek where she'd branded him with her kiss. Fighting the intense need to pull her into his arms and taste those lips for himself.

He dragged in a deep breath, praying he could stay wonderful and supportive and sane. He pulled his hand back from hers and picked up his sandwich.

The last thing he felt like doing was eating...

Riana picked at her chicken roll, more interested in watching Joe eat than filling her own stomach.

He cared about what she was feeling! Was that what having a man love you was all about? Every other guy that had come into her life before hadn't seemed to overly care.

Joe wanted her to be happy? A warmth bubbled up inside her. Wow.

This guy—she tilted her head and watched him bite down on his club sandwich—was like no other man she'd known, all caring and concerned for her. Like she would have imagined an older brother to be, but much more.

She held one hand on her lap, loath to use it. She wanted to savour the sensations he'd aroused in her. How he'd branded her with his touch. How his heat had coursed up her arm and slid into her body, melting her doubts.

It was nice to be loved.

Joe *was* handsome, just in a different way to Stuart's clean-shaven, combed hair and tidy suits way. Joe was rugged, rough round the edges, with hair that seemed to be permanently spiked, but under that there was a sweet and caring man that she couldn't wait to get to know better.

And he was hers. Her fiancé.

She fingered the band on her finger. It felt funny to have it on, but nice, as if she belonged, as if she'd made it…that all those dates, all that looking for the right guy had come to fruition.

She was loved.

Sure, her family loved her but it wasn't the same as finding someone of her own to love her. Besides, with all of them involved with their own relationships, including her mother, there didn't seem to be much of anything left for her.

She took a sip of her orange juice, laying her still tingling hand down next to her plate.

Her family were busy. Too busy to notice her, except to rub in, in sickeningly sweet ways, that she was getting older and was still single.

'Hey, it's okay,' Joe covered his hand over hers, encapsulating it in his warmth again. 'We'll get you a proper ring.'

She shook her head. How could fate have been so wonderful to send her Joe? She couldn't believe her luck at walking into the boutique drunk last night. Fate had been on her side for Joe to be there, and her subconscious sure had done right by her to accept his proposal.

Now, they just had to get to know each other. Spend long hours together in front of a log fire, with a bottle of wine, talking about their lives, their hopes and dreams. And walk in the park, in the moonlight, on the beach. All the things that Stuart had avoided.

Maybe she had it all wrong. Maybe choosing a guy in a club or bar for his looks, his clothes and his suave comments wasn't the way to go. Maybe she had to trust fate.

All those fairytales that her sisters read to her as a kid couldn't be wrong. She'd just read them the wrong way. Cinderella didn't go looking for magic; magic found her.

She straightened taller in her seat. And if fate had chosen Joe as the man for her, who was she to argue?

CHAPTER SEVEN

RIANA drifted into her mother's office. It always smelled of roses. The sweet scent took her back to the early days of her mother's wedding planning career, where playing under her mum's desk in the front room of their house gave her a comfort and a security that she didn't seem to get these days.

She liked coming into her mother's office just to feel the faint echo of it. Mostly she could but today her mother was at her desk, shadowing the mood.

She didn't usually avoid her mother, wasn't hesitant in spending time with her—not having the least bit of fear of her matchmaking skills—but today she didn't know exactly what to tell her about her love life.

She stopped in the doorway, loath to enter. She shouldn't have bragged about the fact that she'd be getting married too, any time now. Her cheeks heated at her stupidity. She'd even been so bold to tell her that she'd expected Stuart to propose last night.

Riana backed out of the doorway quietly.

Her mother lifted her head from her work. 'Hello, honey.'

Riana froze. She didn't want to tell her mother just yet what hadn't happened with Stuart, and how on earth was she going to explain about Joe?

She had no idea what was going on with her fiancé. The more sober she became, and the milder her headache, the more she wondered how any man could propose to a woman who was virtually a stranger. He had to be crazy. Or have an ulterior motive, or be extremely and amazingly romantic.

Lunch hadn't given her any answers.

'How's the photo shoot going?'

She shrugged. 'Over.' And she was sure it wouldn't take Joe long to come to his senses and call off the engagement.

She sighed, letting reality slide through her like hard, cold ice. It was only a matter of time now… That wonderful feeling that someone loved her would be gone. She bit her lip. She didn't want to lose it so soon.

Her mother nodded, eyeing her carefully, a soft smile playing on her lips. 'And have you got any special announcements you'd like to share?'

Riana jerked her chin up.

Her mother moved around her desk and towards her. 'You're positively glowing. You know, darling, I've always known that you were quite okay on your own when it comes to matters of the heart. You've never avoided relationships like your older sisters have—'

Riana crossed her arms over her chest, a chill clawing at her belly. 'Things didn't work out with Stuart the way I'd expected,' she said quietly, not able to look her mother in the face.

'Oh, darling, that's no good.' She patted her arm lightly. 'Well, don't spend too long looking around or all the good ones will be taken. You don't want to end up all on your own, do you?'

Riana's breath stuck in her throat. Her mother had skirted around the subject ever since Skye's marriage to Nick, now it was said. 'Is that a problem?'

'I want you to be happy, sweetie.'

'I can be happy and alone, can't I?' she bit out, her words as hollow as her chest at the thought.

Her mother wrapped her in a soft hug. 'Of course. Sure, dear. If you'd rather concentrate on your career that's entirely up to you.'

Riana clenched her hands by her sides at her mother's tone. She wanted her mother to be proud of her. To appreciate her for who she was, what she did. And she knew that her mother wanted her daughters happy, successful and married. 'I'm engaged,' she blurted.

Her mother pulled back. 'But you said that Stuart—'

Riana met her mother's gaze. 'Yes, I know. I'm not engaged to Stuart. Joe—'

'Joe? That nice photographer fellow?' She hugged her again. 'What a lovely surprise. I suppose you must have known each other a while then—I can never keep up with all the men in your life—I guess that's why he dropped everything in his busy schedule to do your little photo shoot? If I'd known you two had a history I would have supported Maggie more in her idea that he was the only photographer to have. I thought he'd just laugh at our presumptuous request—'

'Sure. Yes. Of course,' she stuttered. She wasn't about to tell her mother that she'd just met the guy. 'One word from me and he fell all over himself...'

'Anyone I know?'

Riana stiffened at the deep male voice behind her. She knew the owner. Intimately? She still hadn't asked him about that.

Her mother smiled past her. 'Joe, I hear you're going to be part of the family. I'm so glad.' Her mother stepped around Riana and drew him into a bear hug. 'Riana is such a mischief, keeping you from us. And fancy considering Stuart. Goodness, she had a lucky escape there, don't you think? You could have lost her.'

'Yes.' Joe glanced at Riana, eyeing her carefully.

Could he see what her mother was saying, what she was implying, where she was going with this? Riana crossed her arms over her chest. He'd have to guess her mother wouldn't accept that they'd only just met.

'I wouldn't have stood idly by, Mrs Andrews,' he stated coolly.

'Barbara, please.' Her mother shot Riana a look of approval. 'So, show me the ring dear?'

Riana put her left hand behind her back, looking towards Joe with wide eyes. Her mother wouldn't understand a plain brass band. She'd have to explain. And no way could she manage that. Cripes, she could hardly understand their engagement herself.

'I haven't given her the ring yet.' Joe reduced the distance between them, sliding his warm arm around her waist and pulling her close to his side. 'It was sort of an impromptu proposal. We were taken by the moment... You know how it is.'

'No.' Barbara shook her head, glancing from him to her daughter. 'Young people today. You know Tara will have a fit to hear about this. She could have given you all sorts of suggestions to make the moment the most magical and memorable.'

'I'm sure she would have.' Joe shrugged. 'But it was special all the same.' He looked down at Riana, a softness in his eyes that made her nerves tingle.

'Well, I hope all this won't distract her next week. She's got a lot on her plate with the fashion show and all.'

Joe swung to face Riana, loath to release her, but he needed to see how she was faring. With her mother. With him. With life. The last thing she needed was more pressure. 'You're going to be busy?'

She nodded. 'Very. One of the dresses this morning didn't go right. I'll need to work on it so it's right for the show on Monday.'

'But I'm sure she'll find time for you, Joe. Won't you, dear?' Her mother patted her on the arm.

'Yes. Of course.' Riana's features softened. She was looking at him with dark, appreciative eyes and the softest smile on her full red lips.

His guts ached. Hell. He was in deep trouble.

'Why don't you bring Joe to dinner tonight?' Barbara said, nodding. 'We've got a bit of a family dinner tonight. Riana's sisters will both be there with their husbands and I'll be there with my Tony. You can meet everyone. We can talk. Tell us how you met originally and how you romanced my daughter.'

Joe's chest tightened. He glanced at Riana. She looked about as thrilled at contemplating the dinner as walking across hot coals. Hell, the last thing she'd want would be being surrounded by her happily married sisters, driving home her failure with Stuart. Or being grilled about him.

'Sorry, but I can't make it,' he offered to her mother. The resemblance to Riana was striking. Dark hair, dark eyes, tanned, only a good twenty plus years older. 'And I have to steal Riana away.'

'Oh dear, really?'

Joe straightened to his full height. 'Yes. We have a prior engagement that we can't get out of. But thank you so much for the invitation, Barbara. Another time per-haps?'

She smiled at him. 'We have them every Friday night.'

No wonder Riana looked stricken talk-ing to her mother. She couldn't be looking forward to having her sisters' good matches paraded in front of her. Barbara wouldn't mean to push her daughter but mothers were mothers. His own was for-ever enquiring after his life and when was he finally going to set a date for his wed-ding to Francine?

'Nice to see you again, Barbara.' Joe stepped backward, snagging Riana's hand and dragging her outside the office with him.

They were halfway down the hall before she tugged on his arm. 'Joe.'

He swung to face her. 'I hope you didn't mind,' he offered, keeping hold of her hand just in case she needed that extra bit of support. 'I didn't think...tonight didn't feel...I figured you—'

She smiled softly. 'Thanks. I owe you. The last thing I wanted to do was sit around with my family all night discussing their plans for children, their holiday des-tinations, their husbands.' She ran her tongue along her bottom lip. 'Or being asked about us.'

He shrugged. 'I figured.'

'Don't get me wrong. I love them all, but not tonight.' She sagged against the wall, holding his hand a little tighter. 'I don't think I could have faced them and all their questions tonight.'

'I know.' He rubbed his thumb over the back of her soft hand. 'So do you have plans?'

She shrugged. 'Like with another bottle of vodka?'

He took a quick sharp breath. No. 'I'd like to cook you dinner,' he blurted. The last thing she needed was more alcohol. He knew where that led and that wasn't where he wanted her to go.

Her eyes widened. 'What?'

'Yes. I'd like to cook you a superb dinner,' he said more strongly, offering her a small smile of encouragement. He could keep her busy. Keep her mind on what was right and wonderful in her life.

She stared up at him. 'You cook?'

He moved closer to her, holding her hand firmly in his, the gentle softness of her doing strange things to his body. 'I do a lot of things. I'm quite talented, you know.'

Riana looked down at their hands. 'I hear that.'

'So? Please say yes. Forsake your vodka for me?'

'When you ask like that, how can I refuse?' she said, her mouth curving into a smile.

His body warmed. She was beautiful. She had to know it. Had to see that when she looked in the mirror, had to realise that Stuart dumping her wasn't the end of the world.

It wouldn't be long now and she'd be right as rain, and give him the shaft. After all, he was bottom of the barrel as far as she was concerned. He could go back to his life, and Francine.

One fiancée was all a man needed. Having two was just asking for trouble.

CHAPTER EIGHT

JOE slipped out of his jacket and threw it on the chair by the door, dropping his keys on top.

Was he crazy? Yes. But for some insane reason he couldn't ignore Riana and her grief. Sure, she was a stranger but hell, if in some small way he could make a difference to her life then maybe he wouldn't feel so damned tortured by his failure with his sister.

He stared around the empty house. He'd half thought of getting a dog, but the road out front was busy. If it got out of the yard...

Joe stalked through the entry to the lounge room. He dropped on to the sofa and propped his feet on the coffee table, closing his eyes.

It would be nice to come home to some-one, but having a dog would be impractical too. He wasn't in a position where he could decline offers of work overseas and what would a dog do without him? He'd have to find a walker who would take every care with his dog that he would.

He shook his head. No. It was safer like this.

He should probably sell the place. It was too large for just one man and, no matter how many decorators came through the house, bachelorising it for him, the house still felt like his uncle's—and it wasn't right that he wasn't here any more.

The clock in the hall struck five. Two hours and she'd be with him again. Riana. Everything about her intrigued him.

She was tougher than his sister…maybe. She certainly wasn't falling to pieces in front of him…thank God. But then, she could easily be a master of hiding her feelings from the world. He'd seen the pain in her eyes, the wild fear on her face, the confusion and vulnerability.

He was doing the right thing. It wasn't as if there was anything more important than saving a young woman's life. Hell. Joe jerked to his feet. Francine.

He snatched the phone up and punched in her number.

'Francine Noelene Hartford speaking,' she said evenly, her voice high and cultured.

Joe ran a hand through his hair. 'Francine, Joe. Look, I won't be able to make it tonight.'

'Oh, darling, no. Surely, not at such short notice.' She paused. 'What's the problem?'

Joe stood up and paced the floor. 'A friend has a problem and...I can't leave my friend without someone to lean on, you know how it is.' It wasn't a lie. It was almost the truth, but somehow he couldn't see Francine liking the idea of him playing sweetheart to a lost and lonely woman who was on the brink.

Francine had a lot of trouble understanding a lot of things about him. Why he chose to work instead of live off the investments he had. Why he helped strangers. Why he didn't shave some days. Why he liked his T-shirts and blue jeans instead of the Pierre Cardin outfits his mother insisted on buying him. Why he preferred living in his uncle's house to a penthouse apartment with views of the harbour.

She tsked emphatically. 'Surely, it can't be that serious.'

'I think it is.' Joe rubbed his jaw, his mind racing through his spur of the moment decision last night to go for it.

If only Riana had kept her expectations realistic with that Stuart jerk. It had to have been devastating for her to be dumped just when she thought he was going to propose to her. She must have really loved the guy to want to marry him.

Joe gripped the phone tighter. 'I really feel my friend shouldn't be alone.'

'So, it's like an intervention?' she lilted.

He sighed. 'Sort of.'

'Well, you could just pass on a couple of phone numbers for those helplines,' she said smoothly, her tone haughty. 'Some problems need professional help, you know?'

Joe stopped at the lounge room window and stared out at the traffic on the street. He could, but there was no guarantee that she'd ring them and she could end up feeling desperate and alone. Could turn to a bottle and who knew what else.

'I have to do this, Francine.' He gripped the phone tighter. 'It's personal.'

'Well, if you choose your friend's problems over *Les Miserables* then they must be serious.'

He cringed. Music at the best of times wasn't more important than another human being, no matter who was going to be there. 'I'm sorry. Look, I'll call you when things get sane.'

'Well, we do need to finally set a date for the wedding. It would be nice to get it finalised so your mother and I can find a wedding planner.'

Joe stiffened. 'Oh?' He shouldn't sound so surprised. He guessed that even Francine would want to move to the next step.

'Anyway, let me know your thoughts on it. I wouldn't mind a spring wedding,' she stated dryly. 'Autumn is quite a nice time for a wedding, acceptable too. There's nothing worse than going to a wedding in the dead of winter or the middle of summer.'

'No.'

She sighed. 'I'd better go and find someone else to go with me then. Are you sure
you'd rather your friend's problems than
my company?'

'I'll make it up to you.' He stared out
at the cars on the street out front, feeling
a wave of guilt run through him. It was the
first time, apart from when his work com-
mitments took him away, that he'd missed
their Friday date night.

'As you should,' she asserted and hung
up.

Joe rang off. He was lucky to have her,
he supposed. She was so practical, so log-
ical and so totally in control of her emotions, and her life.

He glanced at the clock. Time to get organised for the dinner he was meant to be
making.

If Riana Andrews needed a fiancé to
keep her grounded then he was going to

be the best damned fiancé she would wish for.

He could probably get her to see that Stuart wasn't the be-all and end-all. That she had loads of potential. That men would be lining up for the chance to go out with her.

But first thing Monday morning perhaps he would seek professional help for the girl. Her problems could be more than he could handle and an intervention could be just what she needed.

Riana stood on the doorstep, the sound of the taxi fading into the distance. Every nerve in her body was strung out. What was she doing at Joe's home?

Okay, so it wasn't a joke. Joe was seriously into her, serious about being engaged—but she couldn't swallow it. A man just didn't up and propose to a girl like that, one that he hardly knew. *Did he?*

There had to be a motive. What it was, she couldn't imagine… She would have to find out, tonight, before he convinced her body with those soft looks, his warm hugs, and his deep-velvet voice that he really did love her just the way she was.

She lifted her chin. She would have to be careful with him. She couldn't afford to let him get under her skin. And if there was another motive, there was no way she was going to fall in love with him. That would be a disaster.

She didn't need to love Joe, didn't need to love any man. She'd seen her mother after her father had left, with her heart broken into small pieces, living a half life, crying night after night for years. She'd felt the pain herself after her father had left, was left with the harsh reality that her love, her heart, had meant nothing to him.

Never again.

She looked up at Joe's house. It wasn't what she'd been expecting. She'd thought he'd be in some apartment on the north shore, some place that stated his success, that yelled bachelor, a place that screamed playboy rogue with an agenda.

This was not it. The house was quaint and old, with a charm that made her think of small children and pets running around the back yard.

It was probably eighty or ninety years old, with deep red bricks and fittings that looked as though they'd been restored, right down to the large brass door knocker on the solid timber door.

Light streamed out from the leaded windows above the doorway and a small light by the front door lit the short pathway to the door.

Riana dragged a ragged breath into her lungs. She was going to be alone and sober with the man. Her body buzzed from head to toe in sweet anticipation of what lay in store for her, while her mind mutinied.

She rapped the knocker and took a step back, holding the wine in her arms tightly, her cheeks
hot and her mind tossing over opening phrases that didn't sound too dorky, as though she was a teenager on her first date.

The door opened.

Joe was still in his blue jeans and white T-shirt, with a seven o'clock shadow on his jaw that made him look like the rogue she had first thought he was.

He raked her boldly with his gaze.

Riana swallowed hard, stifling her body's wild response to the gleam in his eyes. Sure, she could have dressed up but what would that have said? That she was trying? She wasn't sure what she was doing—this was new territory for her—trusting her subconscious was scary.

Her blue jeans were her favourites, comfortable and clean, but faded slightly from wear. Her soft pink shirt was ironed but simple, something she would have worn around her own place on a weekend. Her black high heel boots were much-loved. And she'd only run a brush quickly through her hair and applied fresh lipstick.

If he wanted to marry her, really, then it wouldn't matter what she looked like. He'd like pure, unadulterated Riana, without all her cute outfits, without the hours of hair and make-up, without all those airs and graces. If he loved her, it would be just the way she was.

'Come in.' He stepped back, smiling as though he was thrilled with her anyway.

Her body warmed. She thrust the bottle towards him. 'I brought this. It's white. I hope it's okay to go with whatever you're cooking,' she blurted. She knew how pedantic some people got over combining the right wine with the right meal.

'Thank you.' He took the bottle, giving the label a cursory glance. 'I'm glad you came. Come in.'

She shrugged, stepping into the entry. 'Well, I figured you were more interesting than the vodka.'

'That's the girl.'

She glanced at him. 'And have a touch more personality.'

'Thanks,' he said, the warm smile still on his lips.

Riana looked away, her blood heating. He was just too cute for her own good.

The house looked as charming and homely on the inside as it had on the outside. The floors were polished, with rugs placed strategically along the entry and hall. A set of stairs with an ornate rail curled up one side, the hall running straight ahead, past an old timber shoebox and coat rack, a hall stand and a chair.

'Nice place.' She moved to the double doors on her left and looked into the lounge room. The brown leather suite looked like a new reproduction of what might have been in the room five or six decades earlier. The coffee table was solid timber, matching both in style and era.

The richly painted lime-green walls made a strong contrast to the bright paintings on the walls. 'You must be doing really well.'

It was a real bachelor pad...neat, as though help came in regularly, but with no specific warmth to it, neglected in its potential to be a charming period home.

He strode past her into the room and put the wine bottle down on the coffee table, swinging to face her. 'I am doing well. Thanks.'

She looked towards the front door, her cheeks heating. 'I'm sorry. I tend to say what's on my mind...in most cases.'

He waved a hand. 'It's okay.'

She placed her hands in front of her. 'And what a nice smell.' She lifted her chin and dragged in a deep breath of the tangy scents. 'What have you got cooking?'

Joe's eyes glinted. 'It's a surprise.'

'O-kay,' she said slowly, assessing his clean shirt, spotless jeans and clean hands without a trace of flour, fat, or food. 'You're not going to try passing off some gourmet takeaway as your own cooking, are you?'

He shrugged sheepishly. 'I'm going to give it my best.'

She laughed. Typical. It was so good to know she hadn't totally lost her ability to assess a guy, and this guy was *not* the sort to be found in the kitchen with an apron on.

'You should do that more often.'

Riana sobered at the intensity in his golden eyes. 'What?'

'Laugh,' he said softly.

The deep rumble of his voice reverberated through her, taking her breath away, as though she'd lost her footing going down a flight of stairs.

She moistened her lips. This man was totally dangerous to her senses.

Should they be alone?

CHAPTER NINE

'COME and sit down in the dining room.' Joe shot her a wink, gesturing through a door adjoining the lounge. 'The meal is all ready...surprisingly.'

The dining room was incredible, with colourful artworks against mauve-painted walls. It was almost as though she could have been walking into a gallery.

The table itself looked solid timber, long enough to seat twelve people. Two settings at one end were made up with fine white china with a candelabra between, the candles flickering softly. Several large tureens filled the space in the middle and a large plate of some sort of flat bread.

'If I could get you to stretch your disbelief for a moment,' Joe said right behind her. 'Then I could tell you how many hours it took to slave over a hot stove and create this gourmet delight for you.'

'I don't think so.' She moved to a seat and sat down, shaking her head. She didn't want him to tell her any lies. She'd had enough from the men in her life. 'How about we just eat…whatever…before it gets cold.'

'Good idea.' He sat down opposite her and picked up the wine bottle that was chilling in the bucket beside his chair. He popped the cork.

'I wanted to ask,' she said slowly. 'Why eat at your place? Why didn't we go out somewhere?' Never had a first date taken her home for dinner.

He placed the bottle down and straightened his setting in front of him. 'I find going out places a bit distracting. You get caught up in the place, the menu, friends you run into and all in all don't end up finding out much about your date anyway.'

She nodded. That was true. She'd have to say that she never found out much at all about a person on a first date. She was too caught up in making a good impression to notice much about the guy.

He started taking the lids off the dozen ceramic bowls on the table, the aromatic scents filling her senses. 'Allow me to dazzle you with the exotic taste sensations of India.' Joe gestured to the plate of bread. 'We have parathas. They're a griddle-fried flat bread.'

Riana nodded. He was obviously the expert in Indian take-away, and probably every other take-away on the planet, in his line of work.

'And this is delicately flavoured saffron rice with peas.' Joe indicated the first bowl, putting the lid to one side. 'To go with our matar panir.'

Riana couldn't help but smile. 'Our what?'

'It's an Indian dish with tomatoes, peas, fried soft cheese.' Joe lifted the lid on the next bowl, and the next. 'And this is vindaloo, for the adventurous. Hotter and spicier than the matar panir. And this is raita.'

'Okay.' Riana peered into the bowl, where cucumbers swam in a thick, creamy white liquid.

'And then, to top it off, some pakoras, both cauliflower and potato.' He swept the lid off a small bowl of battered vegetables. 'And hot mango chutney.'

Riana smiled. He'd gone all out for her. She couldn't help basking in the warm glow spreading through her body. He was doing all the right things.

Joe offered her the serving spoons. 'I figure it would be best if we went self-serve. I tried to get a bit of everything. You like?'

'Yes.' She scooped out a large serving of rice, a small one of the cucumber mix and one of the fried cheese and tomato mix. 'It's wonderful, but I'm easy to please. Give me a pizza any day.'

He looked surprised. 'Me too.'

Riana stared down at her plate, her cheeks heating annoyingly. She was acting like a schoolgirl around him—feeling thrilled at having similar likes—and she hated it. Where was the confident, independent party girl who could keep men at an arm's length?

She took a pakora and a flat bread. 'Are both your parents around?'

'Yes. Must be close to forty years of marriage now.'

'That's amazing,' she said softly. It would have been nice if her parents had made fifteen. She picked up her fork, pushing the cube of crisp cheese across her plate. She speared it, put it in her mouth. It tasted a bit like cottage cheese, but crisp.

Joe served a large scoop of everything on to his plate, arranging the dishes in small mountains. 'Yes, seeing as my dad has spent ninety per cent of that time at work.'

'Workaholic?' she asked, her chest tight. She had no idea about her father's work habits. She hardly remembered the man and didn't want to.

'Definitely. He's in finance.'

Riana took a mouthful of smooth and creamy cucumber salad and closed her eyes, the tangy flavour of the yoghurt mixed with a gentleness of spice permeating her mouth. 'And he didn't want you to follow in his footsteps?'

'He did. Does. But it's not for me.' He brandished his fork in the air. 'I love what I do.'

'And you're really good at it.' She picked up a forkful of the rice with some of the rich tomato base of the cheese dish. 'I hear.'

He glanced at her. 'That sounded like a compliment, Miss Andrews.'

'Jeez, I'm sorry,' she teased. 'Did you need some warning?'

'No, I'm just worried that you may be getting a good opinion of me.'

'Is that a problem?' The rice was amazing. Sweet, as though it had cinnamon in it, yet a little spicy. She stabbed the fried vegetable fritter with her fork. 'After all, shouldn't a girl think highly of her fiancé?'

He nodded, looking at his glass, placed his fork down next to his plate and directed all his attention on her, as though he was going to say something important.

She bit her lip, a strange sense of excitement rippling through her.

He tore his gaze away and picked up the wine bottle, pouring them both half a glass.

The seconds passed. She felt a twinge of disappointment. Whatever it was, he wasn't going to tell her just yet.

She swallowed hard. 'Look, Joe. I'm not sure, okay,' she blurted. 'It seems weird to me that you want to marry me anyway.' She held her wine glass and took a gulp. 'Especially after Stuart and—' Her voice broke. Her stupidity where Stuart was concerned was testimony enough to avoid her.

'Hey,' Joe said softly, reaching across the table and placing his hand over hers. 'You just have to accept that you're a beautiful, talented human being who deserves to find happiness and love.'

She took a deep breath, glancing into his golden-flecked eyes. He was right. She'd have to cut him a bit of slack if this was going to have a chance. 'I thought you said you didn't have any siblings. Is that right?'

Joe pulled his hand back and picked up his fork again, scooping up a load of both rice and cheese stew and putting it in his mouth, chewing slowly.

Riana watched him, taking a bite of the fritter. The batter was fried golden, the cauliflower inside soft and full of flavour as though the process had captured the essence of the vegetable and magnified it. 'Well?' she prodded.

'My sister died a couple of years ago.' Joe took a sip of his wine. 'I'm the only child now.'

'I'm sorry.' A chill swept through her. She couldn't imagine losing a sister. They were both so precious to her, despite their faults, and their perfect husbands.

'Tell me about your work,' he offered. 'Tell me what projects you're working on now. What your hopes are for the future. What your dream gown would be like.'

Riana took a scoop of vindaloo from the tureen that smelled wonderful but she'd never tried before.

'Okay.' Talking about work she could do. She loved what she did and wanted to share it with Joe, wanted him to really know her, to like her for who she was, and to love her just the way she was.

She took a forkful of vindaloo and put it in her mouth. The heat of the dish permeated her mouth, the spices filling her senses and biting into the soft linings of her mouth.

Riana gulped down some wine. She darted a glance at Joe. Was he laughing at her? Did he even care that the dish was eating through her skin?

Joe's golden eyes were on her, his brow furrowed. 'Take some of the raita. It'll take the heat out.'

She shoved some of the cucumber yo-ghurt in her mouth, spreading the creamy smoothness around with her tongue. Ouch.

'I should have warned you.'

She nodded. 'With a bio hazard sign.'

'That bad?'

Riana nodded, taking another mouthful of the raita stuff. But he cared.

She wasn't sure where the time had gone but it was after midnight. Talking to Joe about her life had seemed the easiest thing to do and for some reason he had wanted to hear everything. Her dates usually pre-ferred talking about themselves and their work, their families and their assets, not her.

'I'd better get home.' Riana glanced at her watch and picked up her mobile phone.

She rang a taxi and stowed her phone back into her bag. 'I'll help you with the dishes,' she offered, getting up from the table and picking up her coffee cup.

'That's okay… I have a lady who comes in.' He shrugged sheepishly, putting the lids back on the tureens.

Riana couldn't help but smile as she strode to the adjoining kitchen with the dishes. 'Sure. Well, I'm glad really. I was starting to wonder with all this home-making that you might be—'

'It was my uncle's house. My grandfather's house before him. He left it to me and I can't stand the idea of selling it, or renting it to strangers.'

Riana put down the dishes on the sink. The kitchen was as amazing as the rest of the place, restored to its former glory, complete with wood-fired stove in the corner. Sure, there was a massive gas range and a double wall oven and the cupboards were all solid timber that looked like

Tasmanian Oak, but it still looked perfect. 'It's charming.'

Joe placed the tureens along the bench. 'Yes, but it doesn't really give the impression I'm after.'

She leant against the bench, crossing her arms over her chest. This was it. Where he'd tell her how he really wanted a playboy pad that pulled in the ladies. 'And what is that?'

'That I'm a straight bachelor who happens to like old homes.'

Riana smiled. 'Sure it does, and what's more it sort of says you're open to serious relationships.'

'Oh?'

'For sure.' Riana pushed away from the bench and walked down the hallway towards the front door. 'The house is waiting for a family.'

He ran a hand through his hair. 'Oh?'

She turned around at the front door and faced him. 'I guess we ought to have a serious talk about us.'

'Yes, we should.' He slipped his hands in his pockets. 'When you're ready.'

Riana looked up into Joe's face. He was so sweet and understanding. It was as if he knew that she was tentative about being engaged to a complete stranger.

'Thanks for tonight. It's been great.'

'Yes.' He leant across and opened the door, looking down into her face as though he wanted to kiss her.

She bit her bottom lip, sweet anticipation sizzling through her from the tips of her toes to her lips.

He couldn't have come along at a better time to wipe her Stuart disaster from her thoughts. 'You've really helped take my mind off…things.'

She looked out at the road, the taxi pulling up at the kerb. 'But I've got to ask you…' The words clogged in her throat. She didn't want to think that he was just like all the other guys who just wanted to have fun with her. She wanted him to take her seriously and know that their engagement wasn't a ruse to get her into his bed.

Tears stung her eyes at Stuart's callous words—did he think she was just some toy-girl? 'Are…are you for real?' she stuttered, her voice thick.

Joe stared over her head at the door, his expression unreadable. Slowly he lowered his gaze, to her eyes, to her lips.

Silence stretched between them, tension filling the air, his eyes burning with purpose. Riana's breath caught in her throat.

He leant down towards her.

Riana could have moved away, but she didn't. She was frozen to the spot, every nerve in her body knowing what was coming, wanting what was coming, yearning to feel the magic in his kiss.

His lips brushed hers, a feather-light caress, tasting her mouth, testing her.

Darts of fire shot up her body, slicing through her.

His mouth closed over hers, knowing, wanting, seeking.

She gasped, opening her lips to him, her blood racing through her veins as hot as the vindaloo. He kissed her deeply, taking her mouth, her breath, the strength in her legs.

His slid his strong arms around her, drawing her closer, taking her weight and pressing her closer against him.

Her body raged with desire, her breasts tingling against the thin fabric that lay between them. All that lay between them.

She returned his kiss boldly. She wanted this, wanted his love, wanted to know that he loved her.

Joe's grip tightened, he angled his head and went deeper, until their breath became as one, shared, inseparable to the sensation.

She was caught by his magic, enthralled, and she wanted more, much more, but only if she could keep her heart out of it.

Joe held her close. She felt good in his arms. Hell, too good. Her lips were warm, soft, pliant, giving, and his blood fired to her call.

Hunger drove him. He wanted to know her, taste her, take what she was so generously offering him.

He forced himself to pull back, reining in the urge to take her further, to explore the soft sensuality of her mouth, of her body.

He forced himself to step back, to breathe.

He shouldn't have kissed her. Didn't have the right to feel her lips quiver beneath his. But...she'd looked so sad. So lost.

Her mouth curved into a soft smile. She touched her lips with her fingertips, dragging in a long, slow breath. 'I guess I have the whole weekend to think about that answer.'

She turned and walked away.

Joe could barely speak as she walked down his path. The whole weekend? She wouldn't have work to distract her from her Stuart. Wouldn't have her family and friends at the ready to keep her in touch with her life. And she still didn't believe that anyone could love her.

He stared at the taxi as she opened the door. For all he knew she was heading out to some club to get plastered or home to another bottle of vodka.

His gut tightened. He couldn't leave her alone for the weekend to her own devices. She could do anything. Drink. Drive. Die.

Joe's body chilled. He'd have to keep her by his side no matter what it took until she realised that losing that jerk wasn't a big loss, or until he could get her some professional help.

He dragged in a breath, striding to the taxi and holding her door open. 'I think you ought to move in.'

She looked up at him, her eyes wide. 'What?'

'Move into my place for the weekend. Strictly platonically, of course,' he blurted, his grip on the door tightening. She had to say yes.

'Why?'

He swallowed. 'Because I feel it's the best way to get to know each other.'

'What's wrong with dates?'

He shrugged. 'Takes too long. And all those distractions.' And all that time in between for her to dwell on Stuart and the crack he'd left in her heart. 'It'll be far quicker.'

'Like knowing that I lose the toothpaste lids in the first week of use? Like that I drink a warm cup of cocoa just before bed? That I like my showers long and hot?'

He pulled at his shirt collar. The thought of having her in his shower ricocheted through his mind and body, firing his blood to what all her curves would be like without the clothes, how smooth her skin would feel as he ran a hand down her body, how nicely her body would feel pressed against his. 'Exactly,' he said, his voice deep and husky. He cleared his throat.

'I don't know.'

'Come on.' He shot her a grin. 'We're already engaged. Most couples would think that's the hurdle rather than spending time together under the same roof.' He dragged in a deep breath. 'I have a spare bedroom with a wonderful view over the back yard.'

She nodded. 'You're right. We should at least take the time to get to know each other, but—' She looked up at him, hesitating.

'I have a DVD and popcorn—a spare toothbrush and plenty of T-shirts to choose from.' His body reacted, his blood rushing hot and ready to his loins at the thought of her running around his place half-naked in one of his T-shirts. He had her bad.

'I could stay for the movie, I guess.' Riana shot him a look from under lowered lashes. 'But I think we shouldn't rush things too much.'

'Great. Sure,' he said as smoothly as he could. He'd figure out how to get her to stay longer, later. She might be okay tomorrow and not need him at all.

She tilted her head. 'I have to admit that I'm still hesitant…' She touched her lip as though she was reliving that amazing kiss.

'I promise to be a complete gentleman.' He crossed his chest as though he was a scout, watching her reaction carefully.

She stepped out of the taxi and closed the door, chewing her bottom lip as though she was still fighting with herself over the issue. As though she was going to change her mind and opt for time alone to brood about Stuart.

Joe stepped forward and thrust a twenty to the driver. 'Thanks, mate, but she won't be needing you tonight.'

The taxi pulled away. Joe turned around and faced her. Her blue jeans clung to her curves like a second skin, her breasts thrust against the thin fabric of her shirt, and her soft, full lips made his blood race.

He averted his gaze as she passed him. The last thing she needed was to catch him ogling her like an oversexed teenager.

Joe couldn't help but watch her, mesmerised, as she walked back towards the house. What was he doing inviting her to stay? He could barely keep his control intact when he was around the woman in short bursts, let alone full-time.

He looked towards the heavens and prayed it wouldn't take her long to figure out Stuart was a number one fool and wasn't worth her tears—that it was time to move on. And the last thing she wanted was him in her life.

But could he cope in the meantime?

CHAPTER TEN

RIANA couldn't help herself.

She couldn't risk letting him go just yet. She needed to convince him just how wonderful she was. Just how much he was in love with her so that he didn't go and change his mind on her.

He was shaping up well as husband material. A good job, nice looks with a gene pool with potential, and a house. What more could she want?

She needed a plan to be irresistible. To drive home to him that she was perfect for him. Had he felt the kiss the way she had? Had it rocked his world? Was there a discreet way to find out?

At least now she'd be on hand. She snuggled into the duvet that Joe had

thrown over the couch and tried to concentrate on the movie on the television.

Joe was just so easy to talk to, and be
around. He didn't seem to mind that she
hadn't dressed up for their dinner, hadn't
faltered when she'd picked the food as
take-away, hadn't hesitated to hand her the
second helping of mud cake.

What woman in her right mind would
let a guy she liked see her like that? What
guy wouldn't have a problem with any of
it, especially the second helping of fatten-
ing cake that could add to her figure, as
Stuart had put it, *in a very unseemly way*?

Her subconscious had to be right about
Joe. On closer inspection Joe Henderson
seemed everything a woman could want,
with a shave maybe.

Staying the weekend platonically was a
twist. She hadn't seen that coming. She
probably would have thought faster if she
had, had a few quick questions to fire at

him that would really uncover his priorities where a wife was concerned.

Again, she'd trusted her subconscious.

If she'd thought for a moment, or three, that he was going to put some moves on her if she stayed, she was sadly mistaken. She touched her lips. All she could think of was when she'd be kissing him again, feeling that fire stir deep inside her, and she couldn't wait.

Watching *Terminator*, the least romantic movie of all time, she dug her hand into the bag of popcorn and propped her feet up on to the coffee table next to Joe's very large, socked feet. She was vividly aware of the rest of him right beside her, his spicy cologne just at the edge of her senses.

He had a beer in his hand and she had a wine in hers, only half full as though Joe was going out of his way to show her that he was in no way out to get her drunk and into his bed.

She sighed as the incredibly muscled character took out an entire police station full of cops on screen. Joe seemed perfectly content to sit on his side of the sofa and stare at the television as though she wasn't there, or worse, as though she was just a mate. 'Broken any hearts lately?'

Joe lowered the sound, but stared straight at the screen as though he was loath to miss one minute of the action. 'No, can't say I have. My last break-up would have been about six or seven months ago...and her decision.'

'Oh?' Riana took another handful of popcorn. 'And the reason was?'

He shrugged and dragged in a deep breath as though it was an effort. 'She said I didn't let her close to me.'

'I find that hard to believe.' Riana glanced at his strong jaw, clenched tightly.

'You seem to be the jump into the deep end type of guy to me.'

'Yes.' He stuffed a handful of popcorn in his mouth and chewed slowly. Finally he swallowed. 'With you.'

Her body warmed and she snuggled deeper into the duvet, the kiss still imprinted on her lips and her senses in every magical detail. 'So?'

He shifted in the seat as though he was uncomfortable. 'I guess I just hadn't found the right woman.'

Riana couldn't help but smile. Right answer and in the past tense, suggesting that *she* was the one. She shook herself. Of course he thought she was—he'd proposed to her, hadn't he?

She had to accept the fact that she'd said yes and, more importantly, she had to figure out whether she wanted to go through with it.

She bit her bottom lip. She knew so little about him. 'So, what's your favourite movie?'

He gestured to the screen with the remote. '*Terminator*, actually.'

Obviously. She watched the bodies falling left, right and everywhere—it was a guy thing that she could no way judge his suitability for her on. 'Favourite music?'

He took a sip of his beer. 'I like all sorts of music, but no classical or country. Rock and roll's great and heavy metal.'

'I can live with that.' She glanced around the room for inspiration as to what she could ask that would really get the conflict in natures happening, but the room was devoid of photos, trophies and the like, except for the amazing framed pictures on the walls.

The one over the television was a photograph of a racing car, caught mid corner, the colours of the car streaked. 'Favourite sport?'

'I swim…but I like to watch football and racing.'

She shrugged. 'Favourite food?' If that exotic Indian cuisine was his idea of what he usually ate, then…

'Pizza.'

Riana had to nod. She was sure she had been some big Italian mama in her last life, because Italian was her most favourite and preferred food on the planet.

She scooped some more popcorn up. 'Favourite holiday destination?' He probably liked hiking in the Antarctic or camping in the jungles of Peru.

He put down his beer and turned to face her. 'I have to say the Greek islands.'

Riana shifted in her seat, her pulse quickening. 'I haven't been.'

'You should, it's beautiful. The most blue-blue water, the most amazing people, and such colourful clothes.' He sighed. 'But what I like the best is taking photos of the people that visit there. Catch their wonder and awe, their moods.'

Her belly fluttered at the intensity in his eyes. 'Maybe you can take me some time.'

Joe froze, staring at her mouth as though he wanted to kiss her again. 'Ye-es.'

Riana ran her tongue over her lips, the anticipation sweeping through her like the call of the sirens.

He swung back to look at the movie and took another gulp of his beer and a handful of popcorn, turning the movie back up. 'Sure.'

She watched the Terminator take out a dozen innocent bystanders and thanked the heavens it was his favourite movie.

She wouldn't have known what to do if he'd leant just a little closer to her and brushed his lips against hers, wrapped her in his warm arms and taken her to new heights of passion. She had the suspicion that she wouldn't have minded at all, and that was crazy.

She closed her eyes, fighting her body's traitorous responses to him. So, her questions had got her nowhere but more intrigued with the guy. Could it be possible that he was perfect for her in every way?

No. Her subconscious had to be crazy, and she'd prove it. She just had to ask the right question to reveal that the man who wanted to marry her was flawed in some horrible way so she'd have no recourse but to dump him like all the rest.

He couldn't love her. He didn't know her. And she wasn't sure what made her more afraid. Getting to know him and not liking him, or him getting to know her and not wanting her any more.

She breathed deep and slow, trying to calm her tangled thoughts, focusing on the soundtrack of the movie.

*   *   *

She opened her eyes slowly, the light streaming in from the window almost blinding her. Had the last day all been a dream?

She blinked away the glare. She was still in Joe's lounge, in his house, with his duvet half over her as though it had fallen off the back of the couch and over her during the night.

She froze. She could hear the steady thrum of a heartbeat in her ear, could feel the rise and fall of the human pillow under her head, and could feel Joe's arm wrapped around her, his hand draped over her waist in a charmingly possessive way.

She took a deep breath. Her lungs filled with the intoxicating scent of cologne and pure male. The pit of her belly ached.

The television screen was blue.

She sighed, relaxing into him, nestling deeper into the nook under his arm. It felt nice. Safe. She could almost stay there for ever.

The rap on the door was sharp and loud, echoing down the hall and into the lounge.

Riana bit her lip. Should she answer it or wake him? She looked up at Joe, his head resting against the back, his face relaxed in sleep, almost sweet and innocent. Almost.

She slipped his hand off her waist, sliding off the couch slowly, careful not to disturb him. She picked up the corner of the duvet and draped it over him.

The knock sounded again.

She tiptoed to the doorway and paused. Should she answer the door? What the heck. She was engaged to the man. She could at least open his front door.

What could happen?

CHAPTER ELEVEN

'HEY.' The tall mousy-haired man on the doorstep smiled at her. 'You must be the fiancée.' He held out his hand. 'Glad to finally meet you.'

Riana stared at him, her mind struggling. 'Wow, news moves fast.'

He shot her a strange look of disbelief. 'Of course Joe told me, even though getting details about you has been like squeezing water out of a rock. I can see why now. He's trying to keep a beautiful creature like you all to himself.'

She couldn't help but blush. Joe was so keen on her that he'd talked to his friends already about her? How absolutely, wonderfully sweet of him.

'It's not every day that a mate finally decides to settle down, though one has to wonder how serious you two are—you haven't set a date yet.'

She shrugged. 'It's still early days.'

The man nodded. 'That's the attitude a woman ought to have.'

Was it? She bit her bottom lip. Did couples set the wedding dates right after the engagement? Should she be talking to Joe about when they'd walk down the aisle? He did seem as if he was in a hurry, wanting her to spend as much time with him as possible, wanting her to start on her wedding gown.

The man ran his gaze over her. 'He's a lucky man.' He grinned. 'Would you consider me if you dump the scruffy old fellow?'

Riana tried not to smile. 'Of course.'

'Liar.' The man peered down the hall. 'Is the lad in?'

She nodded, stepping back to let him enter. 'Sure is, but he's still sleeping.'

The man stepped into the entry, looking up the stairs to where the bedrooms would be located.

'In there.' She pointed to the lounge.

'O-kay. Have you two had a fight or what?' He walked over to Joe and shook him by the shoulder. 'Delegated to the sofa already? Harsh, man. You two aren't even married yet.'

'What?' Joe said sleepily, opening his eyes. He stared at his friend and jerked up. 'What!'

'I let your friend in, Joe,' Riana said softly, wary of his reaction to her making herself so at home that she'd answered his door. 'We fell asleep watching *Terminator* last night,' Riana added, biting her bottom lip, waiting.

The stranger gave Joe a kick. 'Way to show a girl a good time.' He looked at Riana. 'Did he torture you by showing you the sequel too?'

'I fell asleep,' she offered. She hoped he hadn't minded her falling asleep. She'd been dead tired.

Riana felt Joe's gaze on her as though he was trying to look right into her soul. She glanced at him, taking in his dishevelled hair, the dark shadow on his jaw, his warm lips and the intensity in his gaze.

She pointed towards the downstairs bathroom she'd used last night. 'I'll leave you two to it, then.'

Riana swung around.

'Jeez, Joe, she doesn't look half as stuck-up as you said—' He paused. 'And she's so much hotter than you described. She doesn't look at all frosty to me.'

She stalked down the hall. Stuck-up? Cold? Joe may have figured that she was a stuck-up designer the first time he'd met her at the club, and on Thursday, but that had changed, hadn't it? She paused. And how did this mate know about their engagement but hadn't had an update on her personality?

She opened the door of the downstairs bathroom. Had Joe decided on her before he'd even met her? Had he had a list of criteria that she was meeting? Was this a head thing and not a heart thing?

Her chest tightened. What would she do if it was true? That the only reason he wanted her was because she matched some idea he had of the perfect woman. *Was she his perfect woman?*

She closed the door behind her. Or was it just a matter of time before he found out that she wasn't and dumped her? She cringed. Like her father had dumped her mother, leaving her crying and alone.

That morning had been burned on her memory. She'd had a nightmare and slipped in beside her mother in the bed. She'd been woken by her father's angry words, been hugged close as the tears racked her mother's body...crying for all the love she'd given, for the love that she no longer had, for the years he'd stolen from her heart.

Her father hadn't come back.

She shook her head. No. Joe didn't seem the sort of guy who would settle on a woman...if he shaved a bit and put on some formal clothes women would be lining up for him. He wouldn't have to settle at all.

Joe had to have experienced love at first sight at the bar and she'd been on his mind ever since.

She lifted her chin, a fuzzy warmth caressing her. He had to have overcome his shyness and proposed on the spur of the moment the other night, to the woman who he knew in the depths of his heart was the only woman he could love. Her!

She smiled and stared at her reflection in the mirror. Her hair was dishevelled and her face way too pale without make-up. Maybe, if love was blind.

She turned on the tap and splashed the cool water on her face. She didn't mind what sort of love spell he was under. His love could be blind, or at first sight, or rock-the-world, as long as *he* loved *her*.

If he loved her she could risk doing anything to prove it—nothing could go wrong.

Joe stared at his friend, Brian, his mind numb. 'What in hell are you doing here?'

'I came to take you to the gym.'

Joe glanced towards the hallway. Brian had seen her. Talked to her. He ran a hand through his hair. 'What did you say to her?'

'What should I have said?' He stared at him. 'I think I said good morning. I told her she was beautiful.' He shrugged sheepishly. 'And that if she didn't want to marry you, I'd be open to the idea.'

His words were like a punch to the gut. 'What?'

Brian leant on the arm of one of his lounge chairs, crossing his arms across his chest. 'I *was* joking.' He eyed him carefully. 'Are you okay?'

'No.' Joe shook his head, running a hand down his rough jaw. Great. Just great. Now Brian thought Riana was Francine. Hell. He'd have to set him straight as soon as possible, before he said something to mess everything up.

Brian nodded. 'I understand.'

'You do?'

'Sure, with a beauty like that I'd be going nuts about other men admiring her.' Brian shrugged. 'I'm sorry mate. I was just—'

'Brian,' he started, taking a deep slow breath. 'This isn't exactly as it seems.'

Brian nodded, his gaze running over the duvet sprawled on the couch. 'Yeah, right.

Whatever.' He put up his hands. 'It's totally your business what you do with your fiancée.'

'She's not—'

'Joe, I should be going.' Riana sauntered into the room, her hair glistening with moisture. 'I'll leave you two to... whatever.'

'Yes.' He could explain to Brian the mix up, could go and see Francine and get back on track with her, could leave Riana to her own devices. Joe jerked to his feet. 'No... I'll drive you home.'

She shook her head, her dark hair brushing her shoulders. 'That's not necessary. I can call a taxi.'

'I have a car,' Joe blurted. 'I'd rather spend some more time with you than go to the gym.'

'Well, thank you,' Brian bit out, leaning closer to Joe. 'But totally understandable.'

'I'll get my bag,' Riana said, swinging around.

Brian punched him in the shoulder. 'Hey man, back off. You're acting super jealous. You'll scare her away.'

He didn't want to scare her. He ran both his hands through his hair, stalking across the room and back again. 'She's driving me crazy.'

Brian grinned. 'I hear love's like that.'

He shook his head. Right. Love. He'd have to set Brian straight, but with Riana around there was no way he could explain what was going on. Hell, he wasn't sure he could explain at all.

He tucked in his T-shirt and adjusted his jeans.

'You know it's funny, from the way you were speaking about the girl you were going to marry, it didn't strike me that there was much passion involved, you know.

Yet, here you are, pacing the floor like a caged animal.'

Joe glared at his friend. He had no idea. 'How about you get going?'

Brian winked. 'Sure. Goodbye kiss and all.'

Joe's gut tightened. The image of Riana's full red lips jumped to his mind, the taste of them lingering like an echo, the memory of them igniting his blood.

That kiss had haunted his dreams.

Hell, she'd been in his arms last night, resting her head on his chest, the scent of her filling his senses, her sweet lips so close. The promise of her made him ache.

He hadn't moved when she'd leant on him. Couldn't. He'd been afraid of what he wanted to do with her, all over, all night long.

Thank the heavens sleep had finally taken him.

He nodded, not trusting his voice, pro-pelling his friend to the door.

'You know, I wasn't sure about you get-ting married and all, but after meeting her…you have my blessing, mate. She's one hell of a woman. You're right. She'd make one hell of a partner and damn, one mighty fine mother to your children.'

'Children,' Joe echoed. He'd made it a point not to talk with Brian about Francine's plan for children. Her plans for her career didn't involve them.

'Yeah, I know how much you want your own.' Brian cocked his head. 'I can almost hear the sound of little feet.'

Joe's breath caught in his throat.

'Well, I'll see you when you—' Brian looked over his shoulder, his eyes bright.

Joe stiffened.

'When you can tear yourself away.' Brian shot him a grin and left.

Joe closed the door and turned on his heel, facing Riana. 'Sorry about that.'

She gave a small shrug. 'That's okay. He seems like a nice guy.'

Joe nodded, his gut tightening. 'Not that nice,' he blurted. Where did that come from? Brian and him went way back. He was one of the nicest guys he knew.

'Are you jealous because he told me I was beautiful?' she lilted, reducing the distance between them.

'I can't believe he said that.' Brian *had* hit on the woman who he thought was his fiancée? Damn.

Riana leaned close. 'You have nothing to worry about.'

No, he probably didn't. She wasn't his. 'Isn't there anything you'd like to say to me?' he asked carefully. Surely she was sober by now. Surely she could see the situation with Stuart more clearly now—just a little. Unless there was a history of mental illness in her family.

She shook her head.

Had she found out he was wealthy and decided she could give up her slick, suave suits and put up with his bottom of the barrel personality? 'I don't believe you.'

Riana's mouth curved into a smile. 'Maggie was right. You are all shy and insecure.'

'What?'

She ran her hand down the side of his jaw. 'Joe,' she whispered. 'You're a really special guy, you know that?'

A shiver raced down his spine, ricocheting into the pit of his gut. 'I—'

He looked down into her face, his gaze drawn to her lips, his pulse jangling. Hell. One step closer and he'd have trouble. 'I don't have anything to worry about,' he said slowly, his mind struggling with the words to suggest the truth without hurting her.

'No, you don't.' She stepped closer. 'Even after meeting your cute-looking friend, I still want to marry you.' She pressed her forefinger to his chest.

Joe stared at her finger pressing against his T-shirt, his heart hammering in his chest. 'You do?' he asked tightly.

'I do, Joe Henderson. I do,' she said softly, running her finger down his chest. 'And I want to have your children.'

She'd heard?

A flood of pure warmth swamped him. Hell. No woman had offered him that. He opened his mouth, but words wouldn't come. For the first time in his life, he was truly speechless.

What could he say?

CHAPTER TWELVE

SHE ran her hand up over the muscles of his chest, a soft smile on her lips. 'Do you love me?'

Joe's body ached. 'I can honestly say that I love that you want to have my children,' he said, his voice deep.

'And?'

'And hell, you're beautiful,' he blurted, grasping her shoulders and holding tight, warring with himself, the urge to seize her in his arms raging inside him.

'Let's talk,' she said softly.

Talk? All he wanted to do was drag her close to him and taste her lips again. Feel her softness in his arms, follow the curve of her body with his hands, with his lips.

'We should probably talk about our engagement,' she offered, her tone gentle, looking up at him from lowered lashes.

'Yes,' he said, his voice husky. He had to do this. Tell her. Now, before another word was spoken. 'Stuart—'

A shadow touched her face, blanketing the brightness, the life in her, as though his name alone tore at the wound he'd made on her heart.

Joe winced, shaking his head. 'Forget about Stuart.'

'Okay,' she whispered, staring up into his eyes with a promise in hers that made him ache. 'I'll think about you.' Her gaze dropped to his mouth.

His breath caught in his throat and a warmth shot through him. Hell.

She tiptoed and brushed his lips with hers.

Touched.

Tasted.

Met the heat in his, fusing, flaming.

This kiss was nothing like before, nothing like what he knew. It captured him. Every sense. Every nerve.

He could do nothing more than take all she offered.

Her soft hands slid along his chest, running up his muscles, making his blood turn to lava, bubbling through his veins, firing hot desire.

Hell. What was she doing?

She deepened the kiss, one of her hands running up his neck and cupping his rough jaw. She wanted more. Was luring him in.

Thought left him.

He wrapped his arms around her, pulling her closer to him, revelling in the feel of her soft breasts pressing against his chest.

Joe pressed her up against the timber of the door and kissed her back, his tongue sensually dancing with hers in the flames of their desire. Hell, her lips were soft, hot, welcoming.

She felt good. But she wasn't his. He reined back his hunger, drew back. 'Riana, we shouldn't—'

She captured his mouth, claiming him, sinking deep into the kiss, tangling her tongue with his. Hell. Maybe she needed to wipe that Stuart jerk from her mind... He could help her with that.

She wrenched up his T-shirt, sweeping it over his head, flinging it to the floor, running her fingers down his back, over hot flesh.

Joe groaned.

Riana couldn't get enough of him.

His steamy looks were enough to set her on fire, let alone the thought of his hot lips roaming her skin, of his hands moulding her body to his.

Joe's lips slid from her mouth down her jaw, down her throat, pressing hot kisses into her veins, stoking the growing fire deep in the pit of her belly.

Joe pulled back, his eyes gleaming with danger.

Riana's heart jolted, sense looming. She should stop, but then, if he loved her... She hooked her hand around his neck and drew him down to her, tasting the flesh of his shoulder, delighting in the guttural noises he made deep in his throat.

Joe's lips found the pulse at the base of her throat, pressed a hot kiss there, his hand running down the curve of her waist and hip and up again, sliding along the flat of her stomach, up her ribs, closing around a breast.

She arched her back, eager for his touch. No man had pressed her buttons as easily and effortlessly as Joe. She turned and found his lips, moaned her need for more in her kiss.

She was beautiful. Joe stroked the fullness of her breast, a hunger burning in him. He needed to know every inch of her, kiss every part of her, worship all of her, all day and all night.

If she needed him who was he to argue? He was helping her out. And he was all for being needed. Francine never needed him.

Francine…

He pulled back, holding her shoulders firmly in his hands, fighting the heat crackling through his body. 'Riana.' His voice broke. He swallowed hard. 'No.'

'No?'

Joe stared at her full, alluring lips as they formed the word, his breath ragged. Comforting her was one thing, this was something else altogether.

He straightened tall. 'No.'

Riana's eyes widened. 'You don't want me?' she lilted, a soft smile on her sweet mouth.

He ran a hand through his hair. Hell. She knew he wanted her. Had to feel his desire for her, in his touch, in his kiss, in the heat blazing in his veins.

Joe took a long slow breath, fighting for control. 'It's too soon.'

She pouted.

'I want…' He licked his lips, the taste of her still with him. He cleared his throat.

'I want to do this right. I don't want to make mistakes. I don't want our relationship to be based on—'

'Oh.' She shook herself as though trying to get her mind to focus. 'Okay.'

Joe stepped backward and crossed his arms over his chest. 'I don't want to rush. I want to know everything about you. I want—'

Riana tipped her head, her gaze intense. 'You want to respect me in the morning sort of thing?'

He sighed. 'Yes.' He snatched up her hand and pulled her forward a step, letting go of her before the touch of her soft skin under his broke what little control he had.

He yanked open the front door. He had to get her away from him before he did something stupid, and sensual, and mind-blowing.

Riana nodded, picked up her bag and moved out of the doorway. She paused on the front step, her eyes on his lips. 'Thank you for dinner and everything.'

He nodded. 'You're okay?'

'Sure. I have a load of work to do on one of the gowns.' She ran her tongue along her bottom lip. 'I'll hear from you?' she asked cautiously.

He let out the breath he'd been holding. 'Absolutely.' He couldn't help but smile at her, at her fragile question, at her beautiful lips and deep dark eyes that he was in danger of drowning in.

Joe watched her walk down to the kerb, pulling out her mobile, her hips swaying, taunting him with what could have been, what he could have touched, what he could have worshipped.

His heart pounded in his chest and his loins ached.

He shook himself. This was crazy. Riana was just a project. Just like any other he'd undertaken to help another human being. This was purely philanthropic.

He clenched his jaw. His attraction to her was just because she wanted him so much. It meant nothing more.

Francine was his fiancée. The woman he was going to spend the rest of his life with. *Wasn't she?*

'Joe, I know you have strange work hours but really a courtesy call daily isn't too much to ask, is it?'

'No,' he said vaguely, gripping the phone tightly. What had he almost done? And was still thinking about.

Sure, Riana was nice to kiss. Not at all like the types of kisses he shared with Francine. The young fashion designer had a lot more passion in her lips than a interior decorator in the Double Bay social set. But that wasn't a reason to turn his back on his real fiancée or his family's wishes. *Was it?*

They loved Francine. His mother was in the same clubs as her. Liked the same music and the same operas. They were becoming bosom buddies, even going to fashion shows and shopping together.

He sat down on one of his steps, staring at the sofa where he and Riana had shared a night, and at the door where they'd shared that amazingly passionate kiss.

The fact that Riana was haunting his every waking moment was because of his sister, nothing more. It was hard to concentrate on anything other than Riana, what she may be doing, thinking, feeling.

Had he done the right thing? When was the right thing the wrong thing? Hell, he'd hardly thought at all the last twenty-four hours—he'd just enjoyed being with her.

At least Riana knew she had him to hang on to, and their supposed engagement—she'd be okay, until he told her the truth about the proposal.

'I have a lot of things on my plate at the moment,' he offered evenly.

'That friend with problems, I expect?'

He tightened his grip on the phone. 'Yes.'

'Well, you know you're too darned nice to these people. They're probably taking advantage of your kindness... I hope you're not lending them money. Or, heaven forbid, giving any to them. You know how easy it is to pick up leeches who just want to be around you because of your money.'

'Some people need a helping hand.'

There was a sharp intake of breath. 'You really don't have to work so much either. I was saying to your mother that you really could afford to take a lot more time off than you do with all the money you have invested.'

'I like my work.'

'Well—' she huffed as though she was ready to take up his mother's lecturing.

'I have to go.' He looked towards the front door.

'Joe. I don't believe this. You know we need to sit down and set a date for the wedding.'

'Yes.' A heavy ache rolled through him. He wasn't ready. He knew she was. His family was. But he couldn't get comfortable with the fact that if he did he'd have to let her into his life, and let her get close.

'I don't know what's wrong with you, you know,' she admonished softly. 'I know you're still upset about your uncle passing away, but it's been years. Using his money doesn't make him more dead than he is now.'

Joe balled his hands.

'Accept it, and move on. He'd want you to make use of his money, marry and settle down and be happy.' She tsked softly. 'Joe, Joe… What will I do with you?'

He stared up at the ceiling. 'I think I had better come over and have a talk with you,' he said in a monotone voice, all feeling wiped from him by his fiancée's words.

She was right. He knew she was. But something about the way she had said it, the way she was, made him feel strange and restless. Empty.

'Well, I'm heading out to spend the day with my friends at the club today and I'm going to my parents' house tomorrow. Monday is all booked up, but maybe I can squeeze you in for dinner on Monday evening?'

'Fine.' He rang off, resting his elbows on his knees and his head in his hands, his mind in turmoil. Could he call it off with Francine? Was this real? Or just a phase he was going through?

Hell. He just needed to know Riana was safe. That she wasn't going to do anything foolish. That she had a firm hold on life.

There was nothing more to it than that. There couldn't be. He was engaged to someone else entirely, and Francine and Riana were like oil and water.

Francine should be perfect for him in every way. His mother thought so. Good family, good job, good social standing and similar interests to his. And Riana was... young, vibrant and irrational.

How could he express this deep ache in his chest?

He wanted to keep her.

Joe stiffened, realisation dawning in his addled brain. He had to tell her everything. He wanted to start again—with a clean slate. No games, no ploys, no desperate attempts to stave off her despair.

Even if he was a rebound affair for her, there was a chance she'd come round—a chance she could see him as more.

Hell. He *was* her fiancé.

Joe let out the breath he'd been holding. She could wait a day or so for him—for the truth—without Francine being an issue against them having a relationship. After all, what could happen in two days?

CHAPTER THIRTEEN

'HELP me.'

Maggie stopped short in the boutique doorway. 'That's why I'm here, though why, I don't know. It's not as though I'm a seamstress.'

Riana waved her words away. 'No. I've got Ang and Becky down in the back room helping me with the gown. I need you to help me with Joe.'

Maggie's eyes widened. 'Ye-es?'

Riana covered her face as though not seeing could wipe out the last couple days of her life. 'You wouldn't believe what I've gone and done.'

She wasn't sure what in heaven had happened yesterday but she knew, in the pit of her stomach, that something was wrong.

She shouldn't be feeling these things about Joe.

How could she? She hadn't meant to. This strange warmth in her chest had crept up on her, taking her unaware. She had barely noticed until she'd stepped into the taxi outside his house.

She'd felt the tingling in every nerve of her body from his kisses, from his touch, felt so much at the thought of him, of staying with him, of belonging with him.

What did Joe feel?

He'd wanted to get her out of his house as fast as he could. Was he scared about the intensity of the attraction between them, or what?

It was so good that he had been strong and made her leave before she fell totally in bed with him, and in love with him.

The other night had been amazing. She'd been afraid to open her eyes in the morning for fear of finding their intimate dinner had all been a dream. She should've have kept them shut so she didn't have to face the reality of waking up in his arms, and wanting to stay there.

She slammed down her hands against Maggie's desk. It wasn't fair. Why couldn't she have just kept him at a casual distance like she usually did?

She bit her bottom lip. Maybe it was okay for her to feel like this, as long as he did too.

But he hadn't said he loved her.

'Let me guess what you did.' Maggie bit the end of her finger. 'You fell into bed with that cute hunk of a photographer who wants to marry you just the way you are.'

'No.' Riana shook her head. 'Yes. Almost, but—'

Maggie frowned. 'I'm getting mixed signals here. Did you make mad passionate love with him?'

'No.' She closed her eyes, the memory sliding over her as expertly as his hands, as his lips.

'So, what happened?'

'We kissed, totally passionately and—' Riana sagged against the front desk. 'I think I've fallen in love with him.'

Maggie smiled. 'Well, that's wonderful.'

She shook her head, the cold chill of her own words clawing at her. 'You don't understand. I can't love him.'

'Why in hell not? Isn't he cute? Successful? In love with *you*?'

Riana jerked to her feet and lifted her chin. 'I refuse to fall in love with someone who could break my heart.'

'You can't be serious.'

She nodded. 'I want you to help me find out all about him, to show me that he's just like every other guy I've let into my life.'

Maggie closed Camelot's front door and flipped the lock. 'That doesn't sound healthy. Dare I ask why? Why you'd want a reason *not* to be with the man you love?'

'I can't *not* find out. This is my heart we're talking about and there's no way I'm going to put it on the front line only to be shot into Swiss cheese.'

'Riana.' Maggie shook her head. 'With love there aren't any guarantees.'

'Well, I want them all the same.' And if she couldn't get them she'd be better off single, safe and alone.

'Why do you need me?' Maggie pulled out her desk chair and placed her bag in the bottom drawer. 'You could do this yourself.'

'I need you to hold my hand.' Riana looked away. It seemed ridiculous. She could handle famous clients, rich clients, rush clients and creatively challenged clients. Why would this be any different?

'You're scared?'

'Terrified.' She bit down on the nail of her thumb. Both ways. She was scared to death that he was a lying, manipulating jerk, or worse, the wonderful human being he appeared to be that she'd let sneak through the armour and into her heart.

'Okay, let's do it.' Maggie sat down at her desk and flicked the computer on. 'What about the girls? Do they need you?'

'I'll go down and check on them later. I've got them busy.' She chewed on the soft lining of her mouth. The gown didn't matter as much as Joe did. She had to know everything.

She'd spent most of yesterday just staring at the gown, running the smooth fabric between her fingers, wondering if she'd really be wearing one herself soon.

'So what is it about Joe that has you concerned?' Maggie logged on to the Net.

'There has to be something that doesn't feel quite right.'

Riana shrugged. 'I don't know.'

'Tell me what you do know, then. We know from the models he's a good-deed-doer. What else?'

'That he loves pizza,' she said slowly, running her fingertips over her lips. 'Puts on a good feed, has terribly violent taste in movies but lives in a grand old home in the suburbs.'

Maggie keyed in a search. 'No loft or penthouse?'

'No.' Riana touched her chest. 'He has a house just waiting for a family.'

'Kids?' Maggie's head snapped up. 'He said he wants kids?'

Riana nodded. 'He wants *us* to have kids.' She touched her lips at the memory of that moment, of the feel of his eyes adoring her, of the warmth that rose up inside her and engulfed her in desire as she recalled his words about her having his children.

Maggie glared at Riana. 'Just marry the guy.'

She sobered. 'What?'

'You should see the look on your face when you think about him.' Maggie rested her hands in front of the keyboard. 'I don't see a problem. He's kind. He eats real food. He wants children and wants to marry you.'

Riana shook her head, the icy claws of her childhood nightmares sliding through her mind. She couldn't trust what she knew, even what she felt. She had to know more.

Riana moved around behind Maggie and looked at the computer screen. 'What's that?'

'That's all I can find so far.' Maggie peered closer. 'It's an article saying how he's built up his reputation, and paid his own way since university.'

'That's nice. But it's all too general. I want the dirt. I want to know if he's a womaniser, who his last girlfriend was. Why they broke up. Why in heaven's name he'd want to marry me?'

Maggie clicked on to several more sites. 'Oh.'

'What?' Riana leant forward, her heart skipping a beat. She didn't want to be right.

'This one is an announcement of his engagement to some interior decorator from a wealthy Double Bay family.'

Riana swallowed hard, her chest tight. 'When?'

Maggie scrolled to the top of the article. 'About six months ago.'

Riana let out the breath she'd been holding in a rush, relief washing through her. 'He told me about her. She was his last girlfriend that he said he'd broken up with about six months ago, probably just after the announcement.'

Maggie sighed. 'So you can go ahead and love the guy to your heart's content.'

Riana cupped her hands together, her neck stiff and her stomach tossing mercilessly. Maggie was probably right. She could, if she was willing to take the risk. 'Search again.'

'I'll need a drink.' Maggie punched in another search. 'Water?'

'Okay.' Riana strode from the front reception area down the hall to the kitchenette, the warmth in her chest growing with each step.

It was okay to love Joe Henderson. He was a nice person who was totally in love with her, wanted to marry her, wanted children.

She opened the fridge and took out a bottle of water, a smile touching her lips.

He'd make a great father, a wonderful husband, and a good friend.

She almost ran back down the hall. She didn't need to waste Maggie's Sunday with a fruitless search for gossip about the man. Gossip was rarely true, or accurate.

She was old enough and wise enough to put her childhood baggage behind her and bask in the love of a gorgeous man.

'Maggie—' she said, catching her foot on a rug. She caught the wall for support, the water bottle dangling from one hand.

'What?'

Something burst from her mind. A memory. Her with a bottle, leaning against a doorway. *Marry me.* Her voice. Her words…

The memory was a knife in her chest, stabbing her heart and twisting. The reality of the drunken moment hit her full force, wrapping her in an icy chill.

'I didn't say yes!' She covered her mouth with her hand, smothering the cry tearing to escape. '*He* did. *I* proposed to *him*.'

Maggie stared at her blankly. 'If *you* asked—'

'Then it wasn't love at first sight,' Riana whispered, her throat aching with the realisation. Everything she'd said, and done, was because she knew he loved her.

What a fool she'd been. She wasn't relying on his love for her, she was relying on her stupidity!

'I don't understand.' Maggie came close and wrapped her arms around her. 'Why on earth did he say yes?'

'I have no idea.' Riana leant on her friend, her knees weak, tears filling her eyes. 'Why in hell would he want to marry me?'

Why would he jump into an engagement with her? Was it that he needed to marry by a certain date to get his inheritance? Wanted to get married before he died of some miserable illness? She quashed the pain in her chest. Or did he want to sire a son by the time he hit thirty-five to carry on the Henderson dynasty?

The question blazed in her heart, consuming her. She'd have to find out, then dump him, before he had a chance to do her heart any more damage.

She'd been crazy to believe in magic. Even crazier to fall in love.

CHAPTER FOURTEEN

JOE opened the front door, half asleep. The game was in the last half but it hadn't interested him. He had too much on his mind.

He caught his breath.

Riana stood on his doorstep, her cream trouser-suit tailored around her curves to perfection, screaming elegant designer, and red-hot woman.

'Hey,' she said, her voice soft and cool.

'Riana.' He couldn't help feeling the buzz in his chest. She couldn't stay away. Hell. *He* was having a hard time staying away from *her*.

'I was just passing by and—'

'How did redesigning that wedding gown turn out?' he said in a rush.

221

Anything to keep him from answering questions he couldn't answer just now. 'I was wondering if you'd get it done in time for tomorrow.'

She dragged in a long, slow breath. 'Fine. Just fine.'

'Would you like to come in?' he blurted. Not a good move. He wouldn't be able to keep his hands off her, or his lips…

She shook her head, looking past him as though she was envisioning what might happen if she did. 'No.'

He shrugged the uneasy feeling off at her tone. Was something wrong? 'So, would you like to go out?'

She bit her full bottom lip. 'No.'

He slipped his hands into his pockets, waiting. The seconds passed. He would have to give in to the inevitable. 'Then what can I do for you?'

She looked at her feet, her cheeks colouring. 'I just wanted to say thanks, for dinner, and the movie and...everything,' she said tightly. 'And for the company, but—'

Joe knew what was coming. She'd come to her senses. The alcohol had worn off. The despair over being dumped had faded and she was seeing things clearly. Too clearly.

He stiffened.

'But I don't want to.' She waved her hand between them. 'You and me.' She shook her head. 'It won't work out. Sorry.'

That was it. The words that he'd been waiting for from the moment he'd said yes to her impromptu proposal. They were out, and a solid measure of her sanity returning.

No one got engaged to a stranger and expected it to work out in the end. Except maybe him.

A chill coursed through his body. His job was done. She was okay. Despite him looking out for her, his questionable movie choice, and those passionate kisses that still burned on his lips.

The memory of her ricocheted through him. A futile fantasy now. The fantasy he'd had of them, together. Of them filling his empty house with small feet and laughter and love.

'Well?' she bit out. 'Haven't you got anything to say?'

He shook his head. Words couldn't convey what he was feeling.

She put her arms across her chest, accentuating the perfect shape of her breasts beneath the light cotton shirt. 'I expected you to say something,' she said, disappointment in her voice.

Joe dragged in a ragged breath. 'I wish you all the best in your life, Riana. I hope you'll keep in touch.'

Riana's chest tightened. Didn't he care that she was dumping him? Apparently not. He obviously had about as many feelings for her as a cat for a tree stump.

She raised her eyebrows, fire pumping through her veins at the sheer idiocy of her proposing to a total stranger and forgetting about it. 'Well, thank you Mr Henderson but no thank you. The last thing I need is to keep in touch with you and be reminded that I went begging for a husband.' She swatted at the air as though pushing the words aside. 'It's not that it's the end of the world that Stuart didn't take me seriously.'

'No,' Joe said quietly.

She lifted her chin and glared at him. 'And I certainly don't feel I need to settle on you.'

Joe jerked his head up, a dark shadow passing over his face. 'You're sure about what you want?'

'Absolutely,' she managed, her throat burning with all the feelings she couldn't possibly share with him. She yanked the brass band off her finger and thrust it towards him. 'Consider yourself dumped.'

She stared up into his face, one question burning in her throat, but the words wouldn't come. Did she really want to know why he'd said yes to her pitiful proposal?

She swung around and lurched down the porch steps, vividly aware of the silence behind her. He didn't even care.

Why he'd even said yes eluded her, but it didn't matter now. She couldn't ask, wouldn't ask. They were over. Totally over.

Dreams like Joe Henderson just didn't happen in real life. She wasn't meant to be loved.

CHAPTER FIFTEEN

RIANA strode across the crowded back room in the changing rooms of Sydney's fashion week's biggest showcase yet of wedding gown designs.

The organisers had deemed that her designs be a part of the opening gala on the first day, giving her an amazing debut and a lot of media attention.

She tried to smile but couldn't.

She didn't care about her aching feet or the questions behind Joe's acceptance to her stupid proposal, or the tearing ache deep in her chest. She'd done the right thing.

There was no way she could have kept a relationship going with him, not knowing that she loved him and his feelings towards her were unknown. It was just too hard to bear, knowing he had the power over her.

She didn't want to be vulnerable.

Her models were slipping out of her designs with Ang and Becky's help. 'Wonderful job, everyone,' Riana said, wishing she could feel more than this gaping emptiness inside her.

The girls were beaming. 'We'll finish up here if you want to go out front and watch the rest of the show, basking in the knowledge that you're the best.'

'Thanks, Ang, I think I will.' Maybe that's all she needed. A look at the competition designs to get her mind off Joe.

She touched her lips, spun on her heel and strode out of the frenzied activity out back to where the audience was.

She scanned the crowded room for a seat.

'Riana.' The nasal whine of a familiar male voice made her freeze on the spot.

Stuart pulled her to him in a bear-hug. 'Riana, honey. Great to see you.'

'Hello, Stuart,' she managed, surprised at how little she felt when she saw the man.

'You're looking fantastic.'

'Thank you.' She gave him a quick glance. He looked pretty spiffy in his black suit and tie. 'You here with your mother?'

'Yes. She just loves these things.'

'That's great.' She looked behind him, scanning the seats for somewhere to escape to.

Stuart pushed his hands into his trouser pockets. 'I want to apologise about last week. I was an idiot.'

She shot him a cool glare. 'For inviting me to your chalet? Or admitting that I wasn't marriage material?'

'I don't know what I was saying...' He pulled at his tie. 'You're a real up-and-coming in the industry.'

She raised her eyebrows. Had his mother informed him of her rise in value? 'Yes.'

'Would you like to sit with us? We're down at the front.' He gazed into her face. 'I'd like to introduce you to my mother.'

'No. Thank you.' She looked past him, trying to hold the avalanche of emotion welling up inside her. She hadn't been good enough last week, but now that she could be in the papers being touted as an innovative designer, she was. Her stomach tossed. The jerk.

'Riana.' He stepped closer to her, looking down into her face. 'Please would you do me the honour of accompanying me to dinner tonight? I have reservations at the finest restaurant in Sydney and I'd love for you to be there with me.'

'Why?' She crossed her arms. 'For a bit of fun?'

Stuart clasped both her hands in his and drew them up to his chest. 'I love you, Riana. I always did, I just didn't realise it.'

'And all that stuff you told me about just being fun?'

'You *are* fun, and witty, and beautiful, and clever.' He pressed his thin lips against her hand. 'And I want to take our relationship to the next level.'

She stared at him. Just what she had wanted to hear, last week. This week she had no idea. He did say he loved her but could she accept him now knowing how he'd felt last week?

If she said yes to him she'd have her house in the suburbs, a family of her own, but would Stuart's fair-weather love be enough? She touched her chest. After Joe.

Stuart followed. 'Tell me I haven't lost you for ever?'

'Stuart,' she said softly. 'I don't know. A lot has happened and I need to think about this. I'm not going to rush into anything.'

'Come on. I know you're still hot for me. Let the nonsense I spouted last week go and come out with me. Be with me. We can pick up where we left off.'

Riana bit her lip. She was tempted just to agree. He'd help her forget about Joe and the emptiness inside her.

'With mother's help I can see now that we could be a perfect couple... Just give me another chance, honey. And, who knows, we could end up going down the aisle some day.'

She swallowed hard. Last week, all she'd wanted was for him to give her that hope, that assurance that they were heading somewhere. Today, it made her queasy.

Stuart took her by the shoulders. 'I love you. I truly love you.'

She closed her eyes. All she wanted was to hear those words…from Joe, not Stuart. Joe.

'Not now, Stuart.' She shook her head, pulling out of his grasp. 'We'll talk later, okay?'

'Excuse me,' said a deep male voice behind her.

Riana's stomach tingled at the voice that haunted her dreams. She turned. 'Joe,' she whispered.

He looked like hell. The shadow on his jaw was heavy, his hair ruffled as though he'd spent hours raking it, his face pale and his eyes shadowed as though he'd sacrificed a lot of sleep last night.

He wore his usual bad boy black T-shirt and blue jeans, standing tall and scruffy, dwarfing Stuart by a good six inches. 'Come at a bad time?'

'No, not at all,' she blurted, her body a crazy mix of hope and fear. What was he doing here? 'I'll talk to you later,' she said to Stuart.

'But Riana,' Stuart whined, glancing at Joe then at her again. Reluctantly he turned and walked away.

Joe nodded towards Stuart's retreating figure. 'So who was the guy?'

Riana lifted her chin. '*That* was Stuart.'

Joe crossed his arms over his chest. 'And he wanted to be with you again?'

'Don't sound so surprised. Sure, I wasn't marriage material last week...but apparently now my designs are getting some recognition I'm back in the ball game.'

'But you said no,' he said tightly.

She gave him a soft shrug. 'I said I'd talk to him later.' There was no way she was burning her bridges until she could work out what she could do to make her feelings for Joe go away.

A muscle clenched in Joe's jaw. 'Do you love him?'

'No.' She shrugged casually.

He dropped his hands to his sides, a softness sliding into his eyes that made her heart contract and her body warm.

'I never loved him.'

'What?'

She waved the question aside. It didn't matter now. Nothing did except getting over loving Joe. She straightened tall and glared at the man who had stolen her heart. 'What are you doing here?'

'I'm here because I refuse to be dumped just like that.'

She froze, her body rigid. 'You want to dump *me* instead?' she whispered, looking up into his face, her chest so tight she wanted to scream. She understood exactly how he felt and who was she to deny him? She lifted her chin and looked him directly in the face. 'Okay, I'm ready.'

Joe flinched as though she'd struck him. 'I don't want to dump you. I want to talk to you about Thursday night.'

Her belly tightened. 'I proposed to you.'

He nodded. 'Yes. I worked out that you must have remembered from what you said yesterday.'

Her cheeks heated. 'I proposed to you when I was drunk,' she stated flatly, a wave of despair crashing through her chest. 'And you accepted. Why?'

'Because I was concerned about you.' He ran a hand through his hair. 'Because I figured you needed me.'

She closed her eyes, her heart darkening with his words. Despite everything, somewhere deep inside her she'd still had a small ray of hope that she'd meant something to him, that there'd been a glimmer of love-at-first-sight at the club.

'You were drunk, distraught over Stuart dumping you, and I couldn't stand by and see you do something stupid.'

'Like what?' she bit out, her blood heating.

Joe shoved his hands in his pockets. 'You had your car keys...'

She shook her head, glancing around the crowded room, thankful they were near the back and no one could hear them. 'What about on Friday? The next morning...?'

Joe pressed his lips together. 'You said you wanted to die. To kill you now.'

'I was speaking metaphorically, not literally,' she bit out, glaring at him. 'You thought I was suicidal?'

'I didn't want anything to happen to you.'

'Who appointed you to be my keeper?' Riana crossed her arms over her chest, fighting the urge to slap him for his arrogant presumption.

'You don't understand. My sister had a bad break-up.' Joe dragged in a deep breath, his eyes dark. 'She drank herself silly and then tried to drive to his place. She never made it.'

The hurt lay naked in Joe's eyes.

Anguish seared her heart for his loss, for his pain and the urge to go to him and wrap her arms around him, hold him, was almost too strong to deny.

She shook her head. 'I'm so sorry, Joe.'

'The world lost my sister, I didn't want it to lose you too.'

His words struck a chord within her. She was nothing to him but another charity case…and so like his sister as far as he was concerned that he had pretended to be her fiancé so she wouldn't do anything dangerous?

'Thanks for telling me, Joe,' she said quietly, her chest burning with pain as though he'd sliced open a wound. 'It helps to understand.'

Though why he'd felt she'd needed that much attention at the weekend was beyond her. She couldn't help but look up into his face at his rough jaw, his totally kissable lips and into his golden-flecked eyes. 'Thanks.'

'I'm not finished,' he said firmly, reducing the distance between them, looking down into her face, purpose blazing in his eyes. 'I care about you.'

Riana nodded. 'I get that.' He cared about every damsel in distress! She swallowed hard, trying to dispel the tearing ache in the back of her throat. She couldn't cope with much more.

'Riana.'

Her heart jolted at her name on his lips, his soft tone, the promise in his eyes. Could he like her? A bubble of hope rippled through her. 'Ye-es?'

'There's more to say. Much more.' He looked around him as though he'd just noticed his surroundings. The catwalk, the upbeat music, the oohs and aahs of the audience. 'Can I see you later?'

'Yes,' she blurted. 'You could.'

'I'll come over to your office.' Joe ran a hand over his jaw, his eyes softly caressing her. 'About five-ish.'

She nodded. She'd meet him anywhere as long as he loved her.

'And I'll tell you everything.'

She watched him go. She would rather he'd stayed with her, watched the show with her, whispered sweet things in her ear and told her everything *now*.

She wanted to know.

Riana swung around and sauntered past the audience, hardly registering them, the spark of excitement at the prospect of Joe loving her surging through her like an electric current.

The only thing to do to cope with the excitement was to plunge into the madness out back. She was sure there'd be more to do to keep her busy.

A woman slipped in front of her, facing her, her tailored lime trouser-suit screaming money to burn, her ivory skin and haughty look stating class and the way she peered down her nose at Riana suggesting snobbery.

'Excuse me,' the woman lilted, touching her tightly wound black hair. 'I couldn't help but notice you with Joe Henderson.'

Riana nodded, a smile touching her lips. 'You know him?'

'Know him?' The woman gave a giggle. 'I'm engaged to him.'

The words hit Riana full force in the chest. This woman—she ran her gaze over her, from her tailored Armani suit to the tips of her heels—couldn't be Joe's fiancée. *She was.* Had been. Riana was the one who Joe had feelings for. *Wasn't she?*

He hadn't said so yet.

Riana bit her bottom lip, ice sliding through her veins. This woman wasn't for him. She was too prim, too pruned, far too proper to share pizza and rock'n'roll. 'And you are?' she managed, her eyes burning.

The woman held out a perfectly manicured set of nails. 'Francine Hartford. Do you know him well? I expect you know him from his work.'

Riana shook the woman's hand, her body chilling as the name teased her mind. She knew that name.

Francine glanced the way Joe had left. 'I was hoping to catch him. I haven't seen him the last few days.' She pointed back towards the audience. 'But I was right up front on the far side… Never mind.'

'You're the interior decorator?' she asked hesitantly.

'You've heard of me?' The woman beamed. 'I do wonder if Joe talks about me.'

Riana nodded, swimming through a haze of tangled emotions. 'Yes.' She'd heard of her all right. Francine Hartford was Joe's fiancée, and had been for at least six months!

Which left her with nothing.

CHAPTER SIXTEEN

'JOE, what a lovely surprise.'

Francine stood by her desk in a lime-green suit that was probably Armani. She loved all the designers, and made a lot of fuss over her fashion purchases. Who made what—he could never tell the difference.

She twirled her pen and shot him a grin. 'I think this is the first time that you've come to my work. To what do I owe the pleasure?'

He stalked across to the window and looked out at the Sydney business district. 'Francine, we need to talk.'

'That sounds ominous. Should I be worried?' She laughed. 'Don't look so serious... It's not as if this last week of distance from me is because of another woman or anything. It was just work and that needy friend of yours.'

'Francine.' He strode across the room, staring dully at the knick-knacks that were meticulously placed along her shelves. He turned to face his fiancée, his gut churning. 'It's about that friend I was helping.'

Francine swept her tall frame into her desk chair, crossing her long legs and laying her hands gently in her lap. 'Yes?'

'Hell.' He ran a hand through his hair. This was harder than he had thought it would be. How was he going to put this without hurting her?

'What?' She shot him a smile. 'You look as though you're going to tell me that your friend was a woman and you've fallen for her.'

The breath caught in his throat. 'Yes.'

She shook her head. 'Come on, Joe. Be serious. As if your mother is going to accept any of those underage waifs that you help out, no matter what sort of model they are, famous or not.'

'She's not a model,' he said evenly, his throat dry as images of Riana popped into his mind. She was far more beautiful than any model that he'd photographed. She had something special about her. Something more. Something that touched his heart in a way that no other woman ever had.

He stiffened. *Did he love her?*

Francine glared at him, her lips pressed thinly, her fine eyebrows arching. 'You're serious?'

Joe slipped his hands into his pockets. 'Deadly.'

She uncrossed her legs and stood up, putting her hands on her hips. 'What? How?'

'I'm sorry, Francine. But, much as I like you, I've met someone who makes me feel...' He couldn't describe it and didn't want to. Considering that it was love was probably not a good idea under the circumstances. It was the last thing he needed to mention to Francine. 'She makes me feel *more*.'

She lifted her chin. 'As if that's been a priority for you,' she bit out. 'You've gone out of your way to keep our relationship orderly and controlled—and I'm fine with that.' She shook her head. 'Is this feeling of yours worth throwing away an advantageous marriage to me?'

He nodded slowly. There was no easy way to say it. 'Much as it pains me...yes. I need to see this through.' He owed it to himself to see where these feelings for Riana led him. If this was love. If this was real.

Francine moistened her lips, staring out at the view, crossing her arms over her chest. 'So you love this girl?'

He shrugged. Did he? The deep ache in his chest at the thought of her might suggest so. The yearning to be with her could be a factor. The thoughts of her tumbling around his head incessantly, haunting him. Possibly.

He hadn't been in love before.

He rubbed his jaw. 'I think I do love her.'

'Don't you think you ought to be sure before you discard everything we have together?' she snapped, pacing the floor.

'What *do* we have?' he asked softly. He'd been wondering more and more why a woman like Francine would settle for a man like himself. He'd never imagined a woman of her social standing and elegance would consider a scruffy self-employed photographer.

She stared at him, her eyes wide. 'I have the Hartford name, and you have the money,' she said as though it was an obvious fact and the reason for them to be together. 'And we suit each other so well. I love your mother and she adores me. Only today we were downtown looking at the latest in bridal wear—' She stopped short and touched her hair, all pinned back to a bun at the back of her head. 'And I'm sure you'll agree that we'll have a beautiful child.'

He swallowed hard. Her answer didn't strike any confidence in him. 'One child?'

She ran her hands over her hips. 'You can't expect me to go through all that twice?'

Joe stepped backward. 'Do you love me?'

'Of course.' She waved her hand dismissively. 'Of course I do, darling. Now, how about you get this girl out of your system—do whatever you feel you need to—and I'll be here, waiting for you when you come to your senses and see that what

I'm offering far outweighs whatever little fling you find on the side.'

Joe stared at her. She was nothing like the woman he thought he knew. Hell. He guessed he'd gone out of his way to limit his time with her so she didn't get close to find out what she was really like. It seemed that the only attraction he held for her was his bank balance. 'Would you love me even if I gave away all my money to charity?'

'What?' Her voice rose in pitch. 'You can't seriously consider that lunacy. Tell me you haven't.'

Joe threw back his shoulders and looked at the woman anew. She was a stranger to him. 'Thank you, Francine, for being my fiancée,' he said gently. 'But I think it's time we both moved on.'

She stared at the floor as though she'd realised she'd given away too much. 'If you're sure?'

'I am.' He looked at her. She'd make some up-and-coming politician a great wife, but not him. He wanted far more in a partner since Riana had come into his life—and she'd be waiting for him.

'Do you want the ring back?' she asked tentatively, staring at the diamond on her finger.

'No, keep it.' She looked more upset at the prospect of losing the ring than him.

She broke into a smile. 'If you change your mind about…'

He nodded, his feet moving of their own accord to the door. He knew what she meant, but no matter what, he couldn't imagine forgoing this amazing buoyancy in his heart for a match with Francine.

He couldn't wait to get back to Riana and tell her everything, take her in his arms and know there was nothing standing between them at all.

CHAPTER SEVENTEEN

RIANA sat behind her desk, chewing the end of her pen and staring at a dozen papers spread out in front of her as though she was sitting for an exam. A wisp of her dark hair hung in her face.

'Looks serious,' he offered, resisting the urge to reduce the distance between them and tuck her hair back. Hell. He couldn't wait until she was in his arms again, until he was holding her, being with her. She was everything he needed in a woman.

She looked up. 'Oh, hello, Joe,' she said, her tone cool. 'They're orders we've received today. There are sessions to book in, measurements to take, fabrics to order.'

Joe shrugged. Not the mood he'd thought he'd find her in. 'Riana.'

She glanced at her watch. 'What do you want?'

He stepped forward, closing the door behind him. 'What's wrong?' Had Stuart been harassing her? By the look on her face, the glimmer of moisture in her eyes, she was upset about something.

He ached to take her in his arms and wipe her problems from her mind, but his feet were frozen to the floor.

She shot him an icy look. 'Well, I've been thinking. I don't think it's a good idea for us to continue this farce.'

His gut somersaulted. 'Farce?'

'Yes. You know, all this nonsense.' She straightened the drawings in front of her. 'You and me. I don't even know you.'

'Riana,' he breathed, his thoughts fading into silence. 'What?'

'I'd like to thank you so much for your magnanimous attention and kisses. They were quite nice. They certainly wiped

Stuart from my mind.' She lifted her chin and met his gaze with cool, dark eyes.

What was she saying?

She waved a hand. 'It doesn't matter. I'm not suicidal. I'm not your fiancée. I meant what I said yesterday. And, frankly, I have other offers.'

Her words struck him. 'Stuart?'

'Yes, Stuart,' she bit out. 'And others.'

Joe's gut contracted, ice sliding through his veins. 'But—'

'And I don't want to know you,' she said evenly, standing up and glaring at him. 'You're really the last person in the world that I'd consider marrying.'

Her words hit him full force in the chest. 'The weekend?' Surely she'd felt what he had. Hungered like he did for the magic that they'd shared in their kisses, the promise of far more in their touches, the connection they'd made with each other.

Her cheeks coloured and she lowered her eyes. 'Well, yes.' She paused. 'That was unfortunate, but enjoyable.' She opened her purse and pulled out some notes. 'I can compensate you for your time and energy.'

'What?' The word exploded from his throat, his mind scrambling to make sense of her words. Did he mean so little to her? Had the hours they'd spent together meant nothing to her but a good time?

'How much would you say would be reasonable? Twenty? Fifty? A hundred?' She flicked notes out of her purse and offered them to him.

He strode to her desk, clenching his fists by his sides, his jaw tight, vividly aware she was staying behind it. 'What in hell is going on, Riana?'

She raised her eyebrows, dropping the notes on her desk in front of him. 'Nothing at all. Let's just say I've come to my senses and I've realised that I really don't have to lower myself to—'

'Bottom of the barrel,' he whispered. Her words that first night echoed around his brain and through his heart.

'Absolutely,' she said tightly. 'And now that I'm an up-and-coming designer I don't have to settle for...you.' She lifted her chin, avoiding his eyes, fingering some gowns hanging off the rack beside the desk.

The enormity of losing her struck him. The knowledge of a life without her twisted in his chest. 'Right.'

She bit her bottom lip. 'You get it?'

'Absolutely. I'm not stupid. I get it.' He stalked to the door, his heart pounding in his chest like a death knell. 'I'll show myself out.'

'Good... Needless to say I don't want to see you again,' she bit out, her voice husky.

He paused, her words slicing through him. So much for love then. He was delusional. Riana wasn't who he had thought she was.

Thank God he hadn't made a fool of himself blabbering about how much she'd touched him, how much he loved her. He'd saved himself some humiliation there.

He'd get over her. Riana's liquid dark eyes were forgettable, her full soft lips something he could forgo, her warm, smooth body just one more body in all the bodies he'd seen at work.

He could forget her eventually—his chest tightened and his breath stuck in his throat—he just hoped it wouldn't take long.

CHAPTER EIGHTEEN

Riana's legs gave out beneath her and she
sagged to the floor, the tears that had been
burning her eyes spilling down her cheeks.

She'd done it. She was safe. She didn't
have to bear being dumped by him, used
by him as a plaything, while he had a real
fiancée. Thank goodness they hadn't made
love…

She shook her head, swiping at her tears.
It wouldn't have been long and he'd have
had her totally and utterly. She bit her lip,
her body traitorously mourning the loss.

Another few months and he'd have a
wife at home. Francine would have the
cute little house, the dog and the children
and she would have had lies. She would
have been the woman on the side.

She covered her mouth. How easily she could have been just like the woman who'd torn her family apart. The only difference was that her father's leggy blonde European had known about *his* wife and children at home.

She should be proud of herself for how strong she'd been in the face of adversity. She'd been the one in control, the one in charge, the one that had made the decision.

She wasn't the victim.

She covered her mouth. It shouldn't hurt as much… She wrapped her hands around herself. This wrenching emptiness that engulfed her would have been ten times worse if she'd waited around for him to cast her off. *Wouldn't it?*

She shook her head. Could their affair have been brief? A quick conquest for him before he tied the knot with that interior decorator. Darn. It wasn't fair.

She looked towards the ceiling. Was it too much to ask for one man to love her totally and utterly? The sort of love where he'd do anything. Walk over hot coals, nurse her when she was sick, hold her close when she was sad, fix her problems for her, and her car.

She lifted her chin, swiping at her cheeks. At least she'd had the satisfaction of seeing the surprise on Joe's face, seeing his shock at her words, seeing his plans come crumpling down around his ears.

She tried to smile, but couldn't.

The door burst open. 'What's going on?' Maggie crouched down beside her on the floor. 'I saw Joe leaving.'

'I dumped him.'

'I know.' Maggie held her shoulder. 'Yesterday, because *you* proposed.'

'I dumped him again,' she croaked, her throat tight. 'He came to the show. Told me about how he lost his sister in a car accident because she'd had a hard break-up.'

'Oh.'

She rolled her eyes. 'He figured he was saving me from myself.'

'So what happened today?' Maggie sat down beside her.

'We sort of made up. I sort of felt we had a future together.'

'Because you love him.'

'Yes, until I met his fiancée.' Her voice broke and she covered her mouth in the hope of stopping the pain in her heart.

'Oh, jeez, I'm sorry.' Maggie wrapped her in a bear-hug. 'I should have chased the guy off with a stick. I should have known you weren't ready for another re-lationship.'

'I wanted him to work out so much,' she whispered.

'I know. He had me fooled too. I would swear on my grandmother's grave that he was as gone on you as you were on him.'

'I'm such an idiot.'

Maggie held her as the sobs racked her body. She hated being weak. Hated being had. Hated being used as if she wasn't good for anything. But at least she'd rejected him first. 'I opened up my heart and just let him walk in and stomp all over me.'

'Come on, you know you weren't that easy. You gave him a bit of trouble.'

She nodded. She had. She should have listened to logic and dumped him totally and absolutely that first time, ignoring her stupid traitorous body and her blind old heart.

She was always meeting the wrong guy, only this time she had let herself love him.

Her chest ached at the thought of him. Of his betrayal, of never kissing his lips again, of never being held in those strong, warm arms again.

She shook her head. It wasn't fair. She'd been just right for him in every way. He was the first man since her father who she'd let into her heart, the only man since who'd broken it.

She lifted her chin. There was one promise she could make. She was never going to love anyone ever again. It hurt too much…

CHAPTER NINETEEN

RIANA stared at her door, doodling her pencil over the paper, her office as empty as her heart. She had done the right thing.

She hadn't slept last night for thinking of Joe, but she figured there were a lot of sleepless nights in front of her. She couldn't imagine closing her eyes and dreaming of anyone but Joe, and that didn't make sense—he'd lied to her, betrayed her.

She stabbed the paper with her pencil. She wasn't one of his young models who needed him to come and rescue her from substance abuse. She hadn't asked to be rescued at all. And if he had decided to rescue her the least he could have done was tell her about it.

She ground the lead into the paper. Was that his *modus operandi*? To rescue a damsel then sweep her into a love affair with him on the side?

Damn, damn, damn. And she had fallen right into his scheme, hook, line and sinker.

Why hadn't he swept her into his bed on Saturday morning? Had he been pacing himself or had it been a clever ploy to convince her of his sincerity?

She rested her forehead on the desk, staring at the blurred lines of her designs. If she'd known he wasn't in love with her...she wouldn't have been stupid enough to let herself fall for him.

She was an idiot.

Now she was right where she'd vowed she'd never be. Alone, with a heart that was cracking in two, yearning for a man that she could never have.

The knock on the door echoed through the room.

She straightened tall in her seat, pushing the wisps of hair back from her face and taking long, deep breaths. There was no way she was going to be anything less than professional at work today.

Yesterday was finished and over. She swallowed down the ache in her throat. Today was a new day and she wasn't going to give him the satisfaction of wrecking it. She lifted her chin. She wouldn't think about Joe Henderson at all.

Maggie's head popped around the corner of the door. 'Are you okay?'

She let go off the breath she'd been holding. 'Yes, of course I am.'

'Liar.' Maggie walked into the office and plonked herself down in the seat opposite her desk. 'Want to talk about it?'

Riana shook her head. 'No. I want to forget about the whole foolish episode as quickly as possible.' And do her best to try to forget what it had felt like thinking she was loved...loving someone.

Maggie eyed her. 'You may be interested to know that you got a cancellation for one of your orders yesterday.'

Riana frowned. 'Already? I thought it would take at least a week for them to work out I was a fraud.'

'As if,' Maggie scoffed. 'No, it was an unfortunate case. Her fiancé called off the wedding yesterday afternoon.'

Riana sighed. 'How sad.' She could imagine the pain the woman was in, if she'd loved the guy as much as she loved Joe.

Maggie shrugged. 'I just thought you'd want to know.'

Riana nodded. 'Just my luck.' If any more orders started dropping out then all the money they'd spent on the photo shoot, the designs and the show would have been wasted.

Maggie leant over the desk and pulled out the order book from under her doodles, pushing it in front of Riana. 'You'll have to slash her off the list. Have you gone over the list from yesterday at all?'

'No. I haven't had time.' Riana flicked open the book, a dull ache washing over her. She should have got to it already, taken advantage of the enthusiasm from the show, but she couldn't bring herself to do anything. 'We'll have to make appointments for the others.'

'Yes.' Maggie sat back in her chair, a smile tugging at the corners of her mouth.

Riana stared at her friend. 'What?'

'Nothing,' she said, sobering. 'Just cross the name off the list.'

'The name?' Riana said picking up a pen and hovering over the list.

'Francine Hartford.'

'What?' Riana's stomach tightened. 'Joe's fiancée?' Her eyes burned and her mind scrambled for the significance. 'What does it mean?'

'That he might care for you.'

Riana spun in her chair to look out of the window to the street, her throat tight. Wasn't it over? 'But I was just another one of his charity cases that he went out of his way to help out.' And use.

'Well. That's sort of sweet.'

Riana swung back to face her friend. 'You've changed your tune.'

'When I heard he'd broken it off with his fiancée… I got to thinking…and I think he might like you.' Maggie leant forward. '*Really* like you.'

'Yeah, right. Sure,' she lilted, trying to squash the flutter of excitement in her chest. 'He was trying to save me from my-self…thinking I was suicidal. What does that tell you?'

'That he could very well be a very special person.' Maggie tilted her head to one side, chewing her bottom lip.

'Maggie.' This wasn't what she wanted to hear. She needed to hear what a using creep he was, not how nice and kind he was. 'You're meant to be on my side.'

'Don't you think it's in your interest to think this through thoroughly?'

'No.' She crossed her arms over her chest. She didn't want to waste another day on Joe, hoping he felt something he didn't. He was just a frustrated social worker playing hero.

She didn't need a hero. She bit her bottom lip. She wasn't Cinderella.

'You love him,' Maggie said softly. 'You've got to do something. He called off his engagement for you.'

Riana jerked to her feet and strode across the room, fighting the bubble of excitement at her words. *Had he?* 'You don't know that.'

Her friend stood up, putting her hands on her hips and shooting her a look of disbelief. '*You* don't know that he didn't.'

'Neither do you.'

'True.' Maggie turned around and meandered to the sofa, straightening the cushions. 'But I think you ought to talk to the man and find out.'

She shook her head. How could she face another round with him? It was all she could do to dump him the first time, and the second time…a third could rip her heart in two.

She didn't want to see his golden-flecked eyes staring at her with that warmth in them. She didn't want to see that rough jaw of his that she longed to run her fingers down again. She didn't want to think of him holding her in his arms for ever and never letting her go.

It wouldn't work.

Maggie punched the cushion and shook it around, dropping it back on to the sofa. 'Riana, you have to face up to the fact that sometimes you have to take risks.'

She bit down on her bottom lip. She didn't want to. She wanted guarantees. She wanted to know this time that he loved her before she made more of an idiot of herself.

'It'll haunt you,' Maggie said gently. 'You don't want to be like your mother and leave things unsaid so you can't move on.'

Riana stiffened. Maggie was right. She'd seen her mother's loneliness, her indifference to her own future because she was stuck in her past, no matter how hard she denied it to herself and to everyone else.

Would she end up like that? Would he haunt her? She swallowed hard, the tearing ache in her chest making her throat burn and her eyes sting. Definitely.

'I don't even know where to find him,' she blurted, her pulse racing. She was going to see him again. Maybe one last time.

'You'll find him.'

She stared at the door. Could she take the risk? Could she find him and face him and be strong enough to cope with the answers…in the small hope that he could feel something more than pity for her?

'You don't want to wait fifteen years to get the courage to face your fears…'

She snatched up her bag. Maggie was right. She wasn't her mother. She was a kick arse designer who wasn't going to be trampled on by anyone, least of all her own past.

She was going to find Joe and grill him about his feelings for her, if he had any at all. And if he didn't love her, fine. She clenched her hands into fists by her sides.

At least she'd know, she wouldn't be haunted by 'what-if's. She could get on with her life, with or without a heart.

Joe stood in the middle of the old theatre, lights glaring on the woman in an evening gown and *faux* furs. He was crouched as though stalking her, clicking the camera, the flashes lighting her further.

Riana's stomach curled. He looked terrible. If she'd thought he looked bad yesterday, today was worse. His jaw was loaded with heavy bristle, his hair so untidy she doubted he'd run a comb through it since Sunday morning, his face drawn.

She approached slowly, nodding to his crew as she went, her hands clenched tightly in front of her. They probably knew the whole sordid story. Their questioning glances said it all.

She pressed her lips together, fighting the heat in her cheeks. She didn't care. She kept her eyes on Joe, breathing slow, counting her steps. Nothing was going to stop her this time from finding out what he felt.

He lowered his camera. 'Wonderful, Eloise. Great job. You're a natural.'

'Really,' the woman bubbled, rushing to him like an enthusiastic schoolgirl.

Getting closer to her, Riana figured she may just be one. Under the make-up was the innocent enthusiasm of a girl no more than eighteen.

The girl wrapped her arms around him. 'You're terrific, Joe.'

'Thanks, but you're the talented one here.' Joe gave the girl a quick hug. 'Go get changed into another outfit.'

Riana froze, her heart leaping to her throat. He was that nice to everyone?

What happened if she was delusional? That everything he had done was just be-cause he was nice, even his amazing kisses, just to make her forget Stuart. *Was he that kind and accommodating to the women in his life?*

Joe put down his camera, swinging around. 'Can we get more light on the right—' He stiffened, staring at her. 'Riana.'

She opened her mouth but no words would come. Just seeing him again made her warm all over, made her eyes burn for all the things that had happened, for what she was here to find out.

'Can we talk?' she said, her throat tight.

His gaze slid over her like warm water, taking in her simple trousers and blouse, his eyes burning. He shook his head. 'I don't think there's any need,' he said firmly as though he'd got over his surprise. 'You made yourself entirely clear yesterday.'

Riana dragged in a deep breath, holding her ground. This was it. No matter if he rejected her on the spot she had to get this out. 'I need... I need to ask you...why you broke it off with Francine.'

His eyes widened. 'You know about Francine?'

She nodded. 'I need to know if you were just playing the good Samaritan.' She bit her bottom lip. 'Or was I an intended fling that you had to have—one last notch on the bed-head before you tied the knot.' She mentally crossed her fingers and toes. 'Or was I something else?'

Joe reduced the distance between them, pulling up short right in front of her as though it took all his will-power to do so. 'You were something else.'

The emotion in his voice slid through her, doing strange things to her heart. 'And Francine?'

'She seemed like a good idea at the time.' He stared into her face. 'I think *she* loved the idea of me and her but it wasn't what either of us deserved.'

'What do you deserve?' Riana asked tentatively, looking up into his golden-flecked eyes, her heart pounding mercilessly in her chest.

She lifted her gaze to meet his.

He cupped her face in his hands. 'You.'

The words were like a soft wind upon her face, sending a shiver down her spine. 'But I was just a charity case?'

'You may have started out that way,' he said, his voice rich and deep and devastating.

'What are you telling me, then?' she asked lightly, straightening tall and looking him directly in the eye.

'I'm telling you...' He brought up his hands to cup her face gently. 'What I should have told you sooner.'

Riana forced herself to breathe over the tingling nerves in her body, the ache deep in her belly, the yearning in her heart. 'And that is?'

He ran his thumb along her cheek. 'I might have started out thinking that I was saving you, but you saved me.'

She wet her lips, waiting for three special words. 'I did?'

'I had settled on Francine because she made sense…and the last thing I need is a sensible marriage.'

She tried to smile, her chest hollow. At least she'd helped him with something. 'I'm glad to have helped you to that realisation.' She needed to leave before the tears welling in the back of her throat overflowed. 'So… I'd better get going then, since my work is done.' She drew away from him, the ache in her chest threatening to break her control.

He caught her hand. 'You're not going anywhere.'

'I'm not?' She swallowed hard. What other torture did he have in mind for her? 'I'm a very busy woman, you know. I just came by to ensure that all my questions were answered so I didn't have to think about the last week ever again.'

'Yes, you do.' He drew her closer to him, looking down at her with dangerously bright eyes. 'Because if the last week of your life was the best week of your life like mine was then it deserves to be re-membered.'

'It was the best week of your life?' she whispered slowly, her voice tight.

'Absolutely.' He looked down into her face, his golden-flecked eyes shining. 'Because, Riana Andrews, it was the week I fell in love with you.'

Her breath caught in her throat.

'Riana, I truly, absolutely, thoroughly, love you.' Joe brushed her lips with his.

Her chest filled with a delicious warmth. Had she heard right? *Truly loved her?* She looked into his eyes and saw his words reflected there, shining down at her full of promises.

He dropped to his knee and took her left hand. 'Please do me the honour of becoming my wife, my friend, my partner in life. Let me share your life. Let me in.'

The breath caught in her throat. 'You've got to be kidding.'

He looked stricken. 'No, I'm not.'

'I'm not rushing into another engagement,' she blurted, holding her hand to her heart. She'd had enough of trying to compete with her sisters.

Joe got to his feet, dropping her hand, his eyes averted from hers. 'No?'

'No,' she said softly, moving closer to him. There was no rush. If it was real their love wasn't going to fade away, diminish or get lost. 'But I'd consider going steady with you.'

His warm mouth curved into a smile, his eyes glowing. 'You would?'

'And in time, after we get to know each other better, if this stays as magical and beautiful…' She stared into his eyes.

He brushed her lips with his. 'Absolutely,' he whispered. 'We don't have to rush anything.'

Riana melted into his arms, languishing in his deep and loving kiss, happy that she'd faced her fears and found the man of her dreams.

EPILOGUE

RIANA put down her knife and fork, smiling across the flickering candles on the table to the man she loved on the other side.

She took a deep, long breath, glancing around at the home she'd made them, all the photos of them scattered around the room, at the flowers on the table, and at the little personal touches that made the house their home.

She couldn't help but smile. She tilted her head at their golden retriever puppy, Arnold, curled up under the table against her feet.

Life was beautiful.

'There's nothing like a special meal at home, is there?' Joe teased, standing up, putting the lids back on the Indian take-away. 'Anniversaries especially should be had at home.'

She lifted an eyebrow, a smile tugging at her mouth. 'You'll have to work out how to actually cook a meal, you know.'

'No-one's perfect.' Joe stared down at her, sobering. He dropped to his knee in front of her.

'What?' Her heart pounded against her ribs, her breath stuck in her throat. Was something wrong?

He pulled something out of his pocket. 'With this ring…'

Riana glanced at the ring in his hand. It was the same brass band he'd given her *that* night. Her heart hammered against her ribs, her love for him singing through her veins. 'Doesn't that come later?' she teased.

'Course it does.' Joe put the ring back in his pocket, his mouth set firmly.

'Oh.' Riana stiffened. Had she missed her window? 'Can I still have it? That ring means the world to me.'

He dipped his hand into his other pocket. 'Are you sure? I wasn't sure. How about this one?' He flipped open a small red velvet box. A round-cut diamond caught the light, its silver setting clasping the jewel like vines cupping a flower.

Her heart fluttered wildly, her nerves tingling, her eyes meeting his, full of love. 'Oh, Joe.'

'Say you'll marry me and share my life with me?' he asked, his voice deep and velvet-soft.

'Yes. Oh, yes,' she said in a rush, wrapping her arms around his neck and kissing him with all the love in her heart, happy to have found her very own happy ever after without worrying about her sisters, her mother, or anyone else.

Finally he pulled back. 'So, do you believe in love at first sight?'

Riana popped the buttons of his shirt, a soft smile tugging the corners of her mouth. 'Only if you'll hold your beautiful body against me.'

MILLS & BOON® PUBLISH EIGHT LARGE PRINT TITLES A MONTH. THESE ARE THE EIGHT TITLES FOR DECEMBER 2004

———————— ❦ ————————

MISTRESS OF CONVENIENCE
Penny Jordan

THE PASSIONATE HUSBAND
Helen Brooks

HIS BID FOR A BRIDE
Carole Mortimer

THE BRABANTI BABY
Catherine Spencer

GINO'S ARRANGED BRIDE
Lucy Gordon

A PRETEND ENGAGEMENT
Jessica Steele

HER SPANISH BOSS
Barbara McMahon

A CONVENIENT GROOM
Darcy Maguire

MILLS & BOON®

Live the emotion

1104 Rom LP

MILLS & BOON® PUBLISH EIGHT LARGE PRINT TITLES A MONTH. THESE ARE THE EIGHT TITLES FOR JANUARY 2005

———— ❧ ————

THE MAGNATE'S MISTRESS
Miranda Lee

THE ITALIAN'S VIRGIN PRINCESS
Jane Porter

A PASSIONATE REVENGE
Sara Wood

THE GREEK'S BLACKMAILED WIFE
Sarah Morgan

HIS HEIRESS WIFE
Margaret Way

THE HUSBAND SWEEPSTAKE
Leigh Michaels

HER SECRET, HIS SON
Barbara Hannay

MARRIAGE MAKE-OVER
Ally Blake

MILLS & BOON®

Live the emotion

1204 Rom LP